D0491999

LANCASHIRE COUNTY LIBRARY
3011814024498 3

LOT

LOT

stories

BRYAN
WASHINGTON

First published in the United States of America in 2019 by Riverhead Books,
an imprint of Penguin Random House LLC.

First published in Great Britain in 2019 by Atlantic Books,
an imprint of Atlantic Books Ltd.

The following stories were previously published, in slightly different form:
"Lockwood" in *American Short Fiction*; "Alief" in *Huizache*; "Bayou" in *One Story*;
"610 North, 610 West" in *Tin House*; "Shepherd" (titled "Cousin") in
StoryQuarterly; "Lot" in *Transition*; "South Congress" in *Midnight Breakfast*;
"Navigation" in *Texas Observer*; "Waugh" in *The New Yorker*;
and "Peggy Park" in *Hobart*.

3 4 5 6 7 8 9

A CIP catalogue record for this book is available from the British Library.

Hardback ISBN: 978 1 78649 783 3
Trade paperback ISBN: 978 1 78649 784 0
EBook ISBN: 978 1 78649 785 7

Printed in Great Britain by TJ International Ltd, Padstow

Atlantic Books
An imprint of Atlantic Books Ltd
Ormond House
26–27 Boswell Street
London
WC1N 3JZ

www.atlantic-books.co.uk

For Arlena and Gary

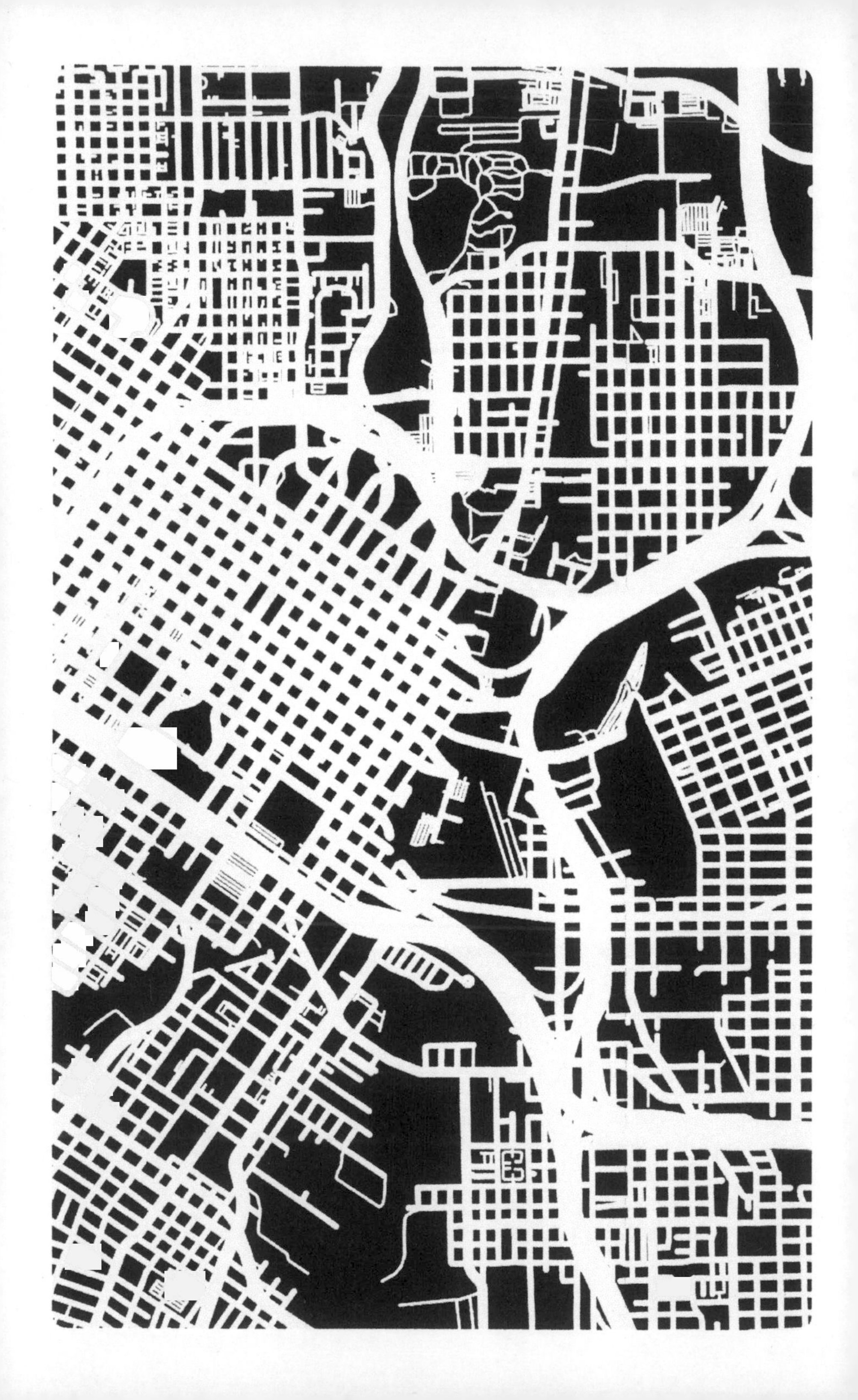

CONTENTS

And how did I
Get back? How did any of us
Get back when we searched
For beauty?

GARY SOTO

and wouldn't it be nice / if things fit / the way they were supposed to / wouldn't that be something / worth dying for.

PAUL ASTA

LOT

LOCKWOOD

1.

Roberto was brown and his people lived next door so of course I went over on weekends. They were full Mexican. That made us superior. My father found every opportunity to say it, but not to their faces. So Ma took it upon herself to visit most evenings. She still didn't have many friends on the block—we were too dark for the blancos, too Latin for the blacks.

But Roberto's mother dug the company. She invited us in. Her husband worked construction, pouring cement into Grand Parkway, and they didn't have any papers so you know how that goes. No one was hiring. She wasn't about to take chances. What she did with her days was look after Roberto.

They lived in this shotgun with swollen pipes. It was the house you shook your head at when you drove up the road. Ma brought over yucca and beans from the restaurant, but then my father saw and asked her who the fuck had paid for it. Javi, Jan, and I watched our parents circle the kitchen, until our father grabbed a bowl of rice and threw it on the tile. He said this was what it felt like to watch your money walk. Maybe now Ma'd think before she shit on her familia. And of course it didn't stop her—if anything, she went more often—but Ma started leaving the meals at home; instead, she brought me and some coffee and tinned crackers.

Roberto had this pug nose. He was pimply in all the wrong places. He wore his hair like the whiteboys, and when I asked why that was he called it one less thing to worry about. His fam couldn't afford regular cuts, so whenever they came around the barber clipped off everything. I told him he looked like a rat, like one of the blanquitos biking all over town, and Roberto said that was cool but I was a fat black gorilla.

He was fifteen, a few years older than me. He told me about the bus he'd taken straight from Monterrey. His father'd left for Houston first, until he could send for the rest of them too, and when I asked Roberto about Mexico he said everything in Texas tasted like sand.

Roberto didn't go to school. He spent all day mumbling English back to his mother's busted TV. Since it was the year of my endless flu, and I didn't exist to Javi anymore—he'd taken up with the local hoods by then—that meant I spent a fuckton of time next door. They had this table and these candles and a mattress in the living room; when Roberto's father wasn't out breaking his back, I usually found him snoring on it.

His mother was always exhausted. Always crying to Ma. Said it wasn't that this country was rougher—everything was just so *loose*.

Ma told her to wait it out. That's just what America did to you. They'd learn to adjust, she'd crack the code, but what she had to do was believe in it.

Meanwhile, Roberto and I walked to the corner of Lockwood, where East End collapses and the warehouses begin. We threw rocks at the cars on Woodvale. Tagged drunks on their porches by Sherman. We watched loose gangs of boys smoking kush on Congress, and I saw Javi among them, and he didn't even blink at me. But that night he shook me awake on our bunk, mouthing off about how he'd kill me if I spoke up. He smelled burnt and sour, like a dead thing in the road. I thought about warning Roberto to keep quiet until I remembered he had no one to tell.

Once, I asked Roberto if he liked it in Texas. He looked at me forever. Called it another place with a name.

Could be worse, I said. You could be back home.

Home's wherever you are at the time, said Roberto.

You're just talking. That doesn't even mean anything.

It would, he said, if you knew you didn't have one.

The first time we tugged each other his father was sleeping beside us. They'd cemented the 610 exit and he'd found himself out of work. It was silent except for the flies above us, and Ma on the porch with his mother, promising that they'd figure it out.

When Roberto finally gasped I covered his mouth with my free hand. We put our ears to the screen door, but nothing'd changed outside. Just our mothers sobbing, and the snores overlaying them, and the Chevys bumping cumbia in the lot across the way.

He'd gotten it all on his jeans, which cracked us both

up—they were the one pair he had. He wasn't getting another.

That night Ma told my father about their situation. She said we should help. We'd been fresh once, too. My father said of course we could spot them a loan, and then they could borrow some dishes from the cupboard. We'd lend them some chairs. The bedroom too. Jan laughed from her corner, and Ma said it wasn't funny, we knew exactly what she meant—we were twisting her words.

Gradually, things began to evaporate from Roberto's place. I know because I was there. I watched them walk through the door. His family still didn't have cash for regular meals, Roberto started skipping breakfast and lunch, and this is the part where I should say my family opened their pantry but we didn't do any of that shit at all.

But it didn't stop the two of us. We touched in the park on Rusk. By the dumpsters on Lamar. At the pharmacy on Woodleigh and the benches behind it. We tried his parents' mattress, once, when his mother'd stepped out for a cry, and we'd only just finished zipping up when we heard her jiggling open the lock.

Eventually, I asked Roberto if maybe this was a bad thing, if maybe his folks were being punished for our sins, and he asked if I was a brujo or a seer or some other shit.

I said, Shut the fuck up.

But you're sitting here talking about curses, said Roberto.

I don't know, I said. Just something. It could be us.

Roberto said he didn't know anything about that. He'd never been to church.

2.

When they finally disappeared it was overnight and without warning. I only knew it happened because Ma hadn't slapped me awake.

I palmed open their door, and the mattress was on the floor, but their lamps and their table and the grocery bags were gone. They took the screws off the doorknobs. The lightbulbs too. All I found were some socks in a bathroom cabinet.

My father said we'd all paid witness to a parable: if you didn't stay where you belonged, you got yourself evicted.

Ma sighed. Jan nodded. Javi cheesed from ear to ear. He'd just had his first knife fight, owned the scars on his elbows to prove it, and Roberto's family could've moved to the moon for all he cared.

The morning before, Roberto'd shown me this crease on my palms. When you folded them a certain way, your hands looked like a star. Some lady on the bus from San Antonio had shown him how, and he'd called her loco then but now he was thinking he'd just missed the point.

His parents were out. We huddled in his closet. His shorts sat piled on mine, they were the only pair left in the house. He didn't tell me he was disappearing. He just felt my chin. Rubbed my palms. Then he cupped his hands between us, asked if I'd found the milagro in mine.

I couldn't see shit, just the outline of his shadow, but we squeezed our palms together and I called it amazing anyways.

ALIEF

Just before they slept together for the final time and before Aja's lover was tossed by her husband, our neighborhood diplomat, onto the concrete curb outside their apartment complex, and then choked, by that same man, with his bare hands, in front of an audience of streetlights, the corner store, Joaquin, LaNeesh, Isabella, Big A, and the Haitian neighbors, James asked Aja to tell him a story. It didn't have to be true.

Before all that, we watched them meet in the market and then wherever they could run into each other. They hadn't spoken yet. Hadn't swapped a single syllable. But we watched them meet in the laundromat. We watched them meet at the corner store. We watched them meet on the sidewalk, a quarter mile from the Dollar Tree. They touched eyes taking out the trash on MLK Boulevard. Aja watched from her window as he parked his car—and she imagined her whiteboy looking right back at her. She imagined him calling our girl down, sticking his shitty blue Honda in neutral, and launching it straight down

I-10, or straight up I-10, or anywhere that wasn't the sill she'd perched on for years.

We watched them bloom like an opera, a telenovela, the sunrise.

When they finally did cross the mountain of silence (after James knocked on her door, thrice, asking about some sugar and cream) they started seeing each other on purpose every day, speaking to each other every day.

Sometimes it was as simple as

Do you have hot water this morning?

No one ever does.

or

So our neighbor, Juana—does she ever put those boys to bed?

No. And that's why her man left her, years ago, for a Puerto Rican.

and even

You know what, it's funny, but I haven't seen the stars since I made it to Houston.

And no matter how long you stay here, they'll never touch your eyes.

They went on like that for months and months. Or maybe it was weeks and weeks.

We never could figure out how long.

James was tall. Pale. Unformed. Like a snow globe or a baker's son. Hardly handsome, if we're honest, but boyish, if we squinted. And the fact that he lived with us at all said something unkempt about his cash flow—way up in the North

Side, on the outer ends of Alief, in that neighborhood stuffed with the back-door migrants, or one among many, hardly a rarity at all. With our Thais and our Mexicans and our Vietnamese. Some Guatemalans. The Cubans.

And yet.

We all knew, just like Aja knew, that he had *something*. In larval form, maybe. Cocooned inside of him.

The sort of thing she'd seen in her husband, years ago. Before they left the island. In Jamaica, Aja's parish sat something like an hour from his, and she'd walked that distance, every day, just to see him. Peasant stock, like the rest of the natives, but she hadn't cared about that; it hadn't meant bunk to her at the time.

She'd been beautiful. The kind of fine that makes you blink. Men all over the coast knew her name, never having seen her, although they'd all heard rumors. And a sideways glance from Aja, along the sandy roads of her town, could send a teenaged boy rocketing home, with his father high-stepping behind him toward his wife or his mistress, to alleviate the beast.

Aja felt the same thing now for the whiteboy. Tried to will it away, but we knew that shit wouldn't fly.

And she found herself on his doormat, knocking on his door.

And he watched her through his peephole, flustered, shouting Come in, come in.

Also, we knew this guy had *questions*.

The whiteboy wanted to know what brought her to

Texas, what the sand from home felt like on her toes. Whether she missed that feeling once she'd made her place in the city. He wanted to know if the air tasted the same. How Houston's smog felt in her throat. He wanted to know how the sunrise fell across her part of the world. He wanted to know about her mother, about her father, her aunts and her uncles. He wanted to know why she married her husband (we imagine him actually asking in bed, after they've sealed the deal, fish-eyed and sweaty) and it must have been then that Aja told him how she'd made it here—that thing we all share—the story of her crossing.

She'd met Paul at the market back home, the way everyone meets anyone anywhere. Aja weighed the tomatoes, eyed the chickens in their pens. Used that time to make plans, wanted to get her ass off the island. Knew the thing about the Caribbean is everyone wants to be there, until they finally, eventually, realize they'll never leave. Our girl knew that like she knew the soles of her feet. So Aja wanted to tweak her English (and not just english, but *English* english, the language of money, the kind we hear in banks) to pull a job as a librarian, or a secretary, or a hostess up north—although really, truly, she'd have mopped vomit at Burger King—because she'd seen on the TV that our public spaces were quiet, and on her island, at that time, quiet was a commodity.

Which is when it happened: she was imagining the sound of nothing when Paul finally made his move.

Her first thought when she saw him wasn't *This is the man I will marry.*

It wasn't *Here is my ticket off.*

She said, Hey, Paul.

Because she'd known the motherfucker for as long as she could remember. Knew him the way we know the sidewalk dips by the complex, or that if we don't lock the doors the kids from Sunny Side'll clean out our apartments.

Paul had moved across the country the year he turned twelve, after his mother poisoned his father, finally fed up with the cheating. All of the men, on that island, at that time, had a mistress, but this did not stop Mom from cooking Dad's favorite dish, oxtail stew, one evening, after he'd left the bed of his other woman. He slipped back into his home, and kissed his wife on her cheek, and sat behind his bowl at the table beside them. Paul's mother told her son he wouldn't be sharing, not tonight.

The incident made an impression. All of a sudden Paul wanted to be a doctor. Hadn't known the reason why his father started croaking, or why his mother watched, for a solid minute, before she made any moves to help. Or why, at the viewing, they eyed the casket for hours, before she spat on his father's forehead and snatched Paul's wrist to leave. But what he did know, or what he thought he knew, was that if there'd been a doctor on the island, a professional who knew what they were doing, maybe someone could've saved him.

Paul could've saved him.

Maybe.

He was that guy.

And with that in mind, he made plans: he, too, started plotting his escape. He studied in the evenings, worked the market in the mornings. Saved the money he bagged in the daytime for night school. Steered his mind away from women for the moment—or tried to, at least—but he lingered over Aja, the way we *all* linger over Aja, and when she came around looking for ackee his was the freshest on the shelf.

In the plan of his life, he hadn't seen a ravenous woman. Not really. But he'd seen one who was faithful, and thoughtful, with good posture. And all of these things were in Paul's head when he asked Aja, one day, timidly, regretfully, if she was busy after her shopping. If he could walk her home.

Of course we got all of this after the fact. Charlie told Jacob, who heard it from Adriana. She took it from Rogelio, who'd been sort of fucking Juana, and the two of them copped it to Nikki down the way. The details are tricky, the certainties muddled, but we knew enough of the story to re-create this: Aja on the mattress with James, in that liminal crease between strangers and lovers.

That's amazing, he said. His finger would've circled her left breast, his chin would've sat on her shoulder.

Your life's like something out of a fairy tale, he said. Like something out of a novel.

You don't know what the fuck you're talking about, said Aja.

Their apartments sat stacked, one on top of the other. When James left Aja's, he took a right toward the staircase, passing four doors, three windows, and the kids—Karl and Dante and Nigel—stroking the fútbol, along with their mothers watching them kick it; and the Guadalajarans on the railing, who leaned, sipping their 40s, reminiscing about adolescence, all lies, mostly; and then there were the delinquents skipping school, smoking cigarettes, nodding along to Joy Division, Ice Cube, and sometimes Selena; until James scaled the staircase, hooked another left, and dipped into the unit adjacent to Benito's, our resident queer. Aja took the same route in the opposite direction when she left his apartment. That happened less often since he mostly came to her. On her way down the railing, though, she would sit with the cabrones, tapping her foot to "Como la Flor," kicking the ball across the balcony, before a word with the women huddled over the veranda. They'd riff on whatever gossip was marinating that afternoon, before she slipped back into her own apartment, at the turn of the evening, where she showered, swept, wept, started dinner for Paul.

In this way, Aja's super-secret liaisons with the whiteboy upstairs weren't exactly a secret at all. They weren't even that scandalous. We're talking about that part of town called Alief, above the sixty-acre mansions, despite ours actually being the worst hood around. The worst. In the years we've been here, we've seen coke wars, turf realignments, the usual school zoning violence, and shootouts—and that one time, in the nineties, with the cracker offing black folks by the Jack in the Box. Some of us still remember the way people walked, like they all had sticks up their asses, like the guy who'd stuffed them there was just around the corner. Mr. Po could tell you about cops cruising the gates. Esmerelda Rivera has photos of the rats as fat as trees.

But the neighborhood's changed. With our not-legals shuffling in, people who don't have time for the violence, people whose only reason for bouncing was to get *away* from the violence, we've mellowed out, found our rhythm. Slowed down. You can raise a kid in the complex. Start a garden or some shit. We make an ugly family, mostly brown and cross-eyed and crippled. Renaldo's son plays spin-the-bottle with Jameelah's daughter five doors down, and Bridgette brunches with Lao twice a month on Tuesdays. Kim Su's niece's marriage collapsed when it turned out she was a stud, and Peter George's son, the burnt one, is doing time for packing. All of the Rodriguez daughters are pregnant, the Williams girl is in college, and little Hugo's hustling for an internship at NASA.

Basically we can't keep a secret for anything. Rumors glide through the complex like vines. But the one person who should've known about James and Aja, the one their opus would've actually mattered the most to, didn't. Or couldn't. At least not for a while.

But when Paul *did* find out, it wasn't from her. She was better than that. It might not be fair to say that she loved him. That might not be true, considering the circumstances. But we knew she liked him enough, or felt indebted, if not protective.

Which might be better than love. It might be easier to put some reins on.

And anyways, she took precautions. Changed her panties before he got home, showered. Set the stoves, cooled the room. Let him kiss her on the cheek. Asked about his day. Massaged the motherfucker's shoulders, when she thought he might like that. Let him take her to bed, although she probably came hours earlier, except it was different with Paul, it was always different.

It just was.

And every night, *every* night, the last words he said were Aja, are you happy?

And Aja always, *always* told him she was.

So we did it. We told him.

We're the ones who opened our mouths.

But not all at once. We're better than that.

Denise whispered it from the lot. Harold mumbled it in the hallway. Gonzalo belched it and Neesha sang it and Marilyn prayed for a flash of intuition.

All of us, the whole complex, watched from the railing, smoking, while Paul bumbled up the stairs in scrubs. Exhausted.

And, the thing is, we liked Paul.

We liked Paul.

We liked Paul.

But we spoke as one. A single cry, and then another. LaToya and Rodrigo and Caramella and Tyrell. In the laundry room, from the parking lot. From both ends of the stairwell.

Your wife is sleeping with the whiteboy above you, we said. She does it during the day, while you break your back downtown.

Straight out. To the point.

When Paul didn't immediately react, we said it again, slowly, pointing toward the apartment.

Gerard cracked his knuckles. LaToya slowed it down.

Right above you, we said. While you work.

It wasn't our first conversation. He knew us all by name. But you'd be stretching the truth to have called us friends, to call us anything other than what we were—just the neighborhood.

We worked our way in as we got to know him.

Appeasing Paul. Pleasing Paul. Fresh off the boat but amiable Paul. We'd seen his type before, had watched this country swallow them whole.

But now, we still crowded around his door, to see how it all turned out. To see if he'd storm the bedroom. Bring her out by her hair. Or maybe he'd turn the pain on himself, fling himself from the balcony, set himself on fire, pull out his very own eyes.

What he did was go home. He locked the door. He sat down to dinner with Aja.

When she asked about his day, he said he'd heard the strangest thing.

We never told Aja it was us, and she never once asked.

We're not the ones who matter here—only her, only her.

. . .

But Aja felt bad about the whole damn thing. Or at least that's what she said. In her weekly haunts with the ladies on the corner, they'd scold her, after they'd gotten the details. The Who put What in Wheres.

It got to her though. That feeling. The one she'd only seen in movies, heard sung on the radio, that weak-in-the-knees, palm-on-your-forehead, *ay*, papi, what have I done.

So Aja was on one of her marathon vents, where she blamed her childhood, her folks, and her people back home, when we finally had enough of it—and we asked her, honestly, why she didn't just tell Paul herself.

We said surely it would be better that way.

We knew that it probably wasn't.

But we watched the neighborhood play out below us. In the yard, Nigel laid a feint on Dante with the fútbol. Mr. Po carried geraniums from the lot. When the ball ended up at his feet, he kicked it so hard across the complex that Dante swiped at the flowers, cussed him out, damned him back to Taiwan.

Aja lit another cigarette. She watched the street too.

Maybe, she said, and even then we regretted it.

No one knows exactly how it all went down, but we'll do our best:

Aja, was all he said when he caught them. He'd actually

walked in on them right after the act. She'd never tell us what it was like, but scandal transcends languages, cultures, generations.

There was the shock on their faces at actually being caught. The shock on his. Confusion. Bewilderment.

And then everything else.

All we know for certain is how he'd said her name.

All breathy, like it was his final word.

The investigation wasn't much, which is to say there wasn't really an investigation. Sure, the same cops we always get showed their faces. Officer Ramirez, Officer Brown, Officer Onlyamonthontheforce. Said hello to everybody, waved up and down the complex, gave a long whistle once they finally reached the body.

Ramirez knocked on doors while Benito and Kim stood over Paul, who hadn't packed up his shit, or caught the bus, or sped halfway across the state (even with the killing crusting on his own two hands, he wasn't a bad guy. We couldn't have called him a bad guy).

You all right, we asked, and Paul only nodded.

Ramirez hit every apartment. But of course there weren't any witnesses. And of course nobody'd seen the signs, but he wanted to get it on paper.

Documentation, he said. That's how we do it in this country.

A noxious joke. But we laughed regardless. Ha! Ha ha! Ha.

. . .

Eventually they made it to Aja's. Told her she didn't have to report anything then, but at some point they'd be bringing her in.

She said that was fine but to fuck off in the meantime.

The medics passed through to flip James on a stretcher.

The whole thing was done in like an hour, maybe two.

A little while afterwards, the hallway filled up again, with all of us who hadn't had a story just moments before. Shouting all at once. Riffing on how this one couldn't believe that the cops had come, how that one had no idea where her papers were *anyways*, how the other one had a warrant for his *own* arrest, and wasn't he glad that they weren't there for him.

We lamented Paul. We chastised Aja. We shook our heads at the whole damn thing.

Whiteboy slumming, what could you expect.

It was dark before everyone slunk back home. Shouting and laughing and filling in the blanks.

She moved out soon after that. Did it during the day. We only caught her because she'd been taking out the trash.

There was our girl, scaling the staircase, in sweatpants

and a sweater. Makeup smeared halfway down her cheeks. Hair here there and everywhere.

But beautiful, still.

We asked where she was going. She said she didn't know.

Home, we said, and she shook her head.

Just somewhere else.

And so Aja wasn't present for James's funeral. A week before they closed the case, long after Paul was in chains.

No family flew down to claim the body. No crying mother at the coroner's. No wincing aunts decrying our ghetto. No protests, no media, not even a gaggle of friends.

James's departure was a quiet one, or it certainly would've been. Because his desires were untainted. Self-propelled. Without accommodation.

He was, despite everything, still one of us.

So we put our heads together.

We pulled the change from nowhere.

We plugged Big A for the quarters under his bed. We asked Mr. Po for some of his flower money. We drilled Gonzalo and Erica for a little of their comp-pay. We pestered Juana for some alimony, and Rogelio for his overtime, and the three Ramirez daughters for their baby shower stash. We poked Charlie for those international checks, Adriana for her allowance, Neesha for her government check, and Dante for his lunch money. Nigel and Karl for the pennies they stole. LaToya for those side jobs, Benito for his Hazelwood, and Hugo for the paystubs he'd been cashing on the West Side.

We hung streamers from the balcony. Grilled wings from the first floor. Plugged speakers, pitched goalposts, sipped liquor, raised arms.

And from the viejas to the juniors to the Filipinos to the black folks, we danced, danced, danced, to the tune of that story, their story, his story, our story, because we'd been gifted it, we'd birthed it, we'd pulled it from the ashes. Aja was Aja and Paul was Paul and James was James and James was Paul and Aja was James and they were us, and we told it, remixed it, we danced it from the stairwell, and we hung it from the laundry, and we shook it from the second floor, until our words had run out, until our music ran dry, and Five-0 shut it down on account of the noise.

610 NORTH, 610 WEST

1.

For a while our father kept this other woman in the Heights. It was tough luck seeing him most nights at best. He'd snatch his keys from the kitchen counter, nod at all of us at once, spit something about how he had business to handle, and of course he never thought to tell us what it could be but we figured it out. We adjusted accordingly.

This was back when Ma's sisters still checked on her weekly: phone calls after dinner, occasional visits on Sunday. Before they finally cut her off for hooking up with a spic. They told Ma it was one thing to live with a liar, and another to give him babies, but coming home to those lies every night was demeaning.

At the end of the day, they couldn't accept it.

At the end of the day, Ma told them they didn't have to.

But those first few weeks she waited up for our father, because she didn't want to see it and you know how that goes. At work she kept busy counting tips by the register. Refilling baskets of silverware. At home, at night, she kept Javi and Jan and me starving while she cleaned the place solo, wiping and mopping and washing the linoleum. Then the four of us sat around bowls full of whatever'd been left in the kitchen—pots of chicken and chorizo and beans on the burners—and we'd stare at the plastic with our hands in our laps like they'd show us whoever kept Ma's man out in the world.

She's gotta be white, said Javi. He's already got a nigga. Otherwise, there's no fucking point.

She could be Chinese, I said. Or mixed. She could be like us.

Why the fuck would he leave home to go back home.

Doesn't matter what she looks like, said Jan. The point is that he's gone.

My brother waved that away. He didn't even look up.

We spent whole days guessing. At what she looked like, where she stayed. Javi swore our father's puta was a model. Or an actress. But for the longest time I held out for something more domestic.

I painted her as a hairdresser. Maybe a dentist. A vet, although a year ago our father'd drowned the dog because none of us ever walked it. These conversations usually ended up with Javi smacking me down, pinching the fat on my ribs. Wondering how I could be so stupid.

Whenever summer hit, Ma kept us in the restaurant. We lived on the building's second floor and ran the business below. But whenever June hit, her usual staff begged off, blaming the lack of AC and ice water on hand, so Houston's sun had them out drinking 40s on Navigation, which left Javi and me sweeping, killing roaches, stomping the tile lining the doorway. Jan disappeared into the neighborhood for hours, citing work, and then friends, until she stopped giving reasons altogether. Sometimes Ma just stood at the register, watching the two of us, and I'd wonder whether she saw her sons or replicas of her husband. But it only lasted a minute before her brow completely settled, and she'd point toward some invisible spot we'd missed right under the table.

Why the fuck would he be tripping over a mutt, said Javi, and when I didn't have an answer for that he chalked it up to dumbness.

She's definitely white, said Javi. She's definitely pale all over.

And she's probably got a fat ass too, he said.

Eventually Ma spoke up. Caught our father in the doorway, called him a bastard to his face. A wetback. And the one night my brother finally opened his mouth over breakfast, asking Ma why she didn't just drop him already, our mother reared back her elbow, crashing her palm into his cheek, before she settled her fingers right back onto the cutlery.

Javi slumped across the wood, crying into his knuckles. I sat beside him, kicking at the chair.

It was the last time Ma ever hit him. The one time I'd see him cry. But when our father saw the bruise in the morning, Javi only told him he'd had a scrap.

We were prepping in the back kitchen. Ma was still in her bedroom upstairs. We'd heard the shouts when he made it home late last night, the fists smacking against the wall.

After enough time had passed that I'd forgotten about the lie, our father asked Javi if he'd won.

My brother curled his lips, testing the wound with his tongue.

Of course, he said. No doubt.

And our father cracked his wrists, staring into the sink.

Let me tell you a secret, he said. That's all that really matters.

2.

Nowadays she doesn't come across as one of those women who dupe themselves, but back then Ma wore it all on her face. That was the worst thing. You could spot it across the block. And not because he left us—that shit could happen to anyone; and it *did* end up happening to us, eventually—but for the years leading up to the break, she thought she'd be the one to reel him back in.

My father was a handsome man. Wore his skin like a sunburnt peach. He was someone who could sing, who actually had a voice worth listening to. He'd pace around the restaurant, beating his stomach like a drum, humming the corridos he'd never taught us way back when. He'd flip me over his shoulder if he found me at the sink, carrying me away, convinced that it was the last place a boy needed to be.

Es solo para mujeres y maricones, he said, because the real men of the kitchen were out killing pigs or whatever.

But you, he said, you're like your old man. Hierba mala nunca muere.

Then he'd drop me back onto my toes, kicking my ass with the flat of his foot.

Ma said that kind of wildness put boys in the dirt. But then our father'd grab her, too. Back when things were still good you wouldn't catch them again for hours after that, which left Javi and me up front, tending to the customers, counting receipts.

But the funny thing is, Ma actually had options—I can't even tell you how many men coasted through the doors, interested in her.

Bald and young and old and hooded and thick and loose and hard, they'd whistle me to their tables. Offer me tips if I reeled her over. Once Ma found out, she told me to always, always agree—free money didn't get any easier. Sometimes she even slipped me an extra bill. Then she'd walk their way, beaming, asking if they'd enjoyed their tacos. Maybe setting a palm on a shoulder. Maybe laughing at a joke. And when the conversation turned toward her, and how she was doing, and how was my father, she'd wrap a hand across her chest, bringing the conversation to an end.

Ma shot all of them down. But never irreparably. Just enough to have them thinking they were always in striking distance. If they'd paid me more, I could've told them it wasn't worth it—but tell someone they want an impossible thing and they'll act like you've put out the sun.

3.

Most weekends back then we caught the first bus to the market.

Javi slept in. Jan stayed out. Ma and I rode through East End, past Wayland, over Main, until we hit 610 headed straight toward Airline. You never saw any other niggas on the line—hair aside, I usually passed. But Ma looked like the thing that didn't belong. All the poblanos stared like we'd touched down from Mars.

One time this guy in an Astros cap actually grabbed her shoulder, told her the route downtown was the other way, pointing back toward Fannin.

In case you mistake, he said, smiling. His teeth were yellow, chipped around the cheeks.

He clearly meant well. Ma returned the smile. She wrapped her fingers around his hand, squeezing at the wrist.

Sí claro, she said, pero no tienen lo que estoy buscando.

And the man's face folded. He sat back down. The rest of the bus shut the fuck up along with him.

The market'd been around for decades, tucked way out in Alief, where motherfuckers were born, lived, and died without coughing a word of English. The whole place smelled like rotten bananas and smog, and you couldn't stretch your hands without brushing somebody's junk. But through the elbows in our noses and the sandals stomping our toes, Ma wore a different face. The one she faked for her suitors.

Only now it was genuine. She really meant that shit. Whenever we hit the first tents, and their humidity kissed our cheeks, I felt her shoulders drop beside me like this weight had just slid off her.

She'd flirt with the little man hawking avocados. She cooed her pidgin Spanish at the homeless kids sitting at the edge of the tents. We watched sons chop chickens in the shacks behind the market, allowing the birds to pirouette in their hands before they finally snapped their necks. The women at the bakery eventually called her doña, growing warmer once they decided we'd be regulars.

Mariachis shouted choruses to stragglers in the plaza. My father would've groaned, but Ma nodded along. Like she was the one who'd grown up with it. Bouncing in her flip-flops. Slapping at her thighs. And, once, this kid actually offered her his hand, and Ma'd smiled slowly, widely, before she reached out and took it—and then all of a sudden they were dancing, swaying, slipping and dipping across the sanded patio.

When her laughter finally came, it drenched the crowd. Some vendors on break clapped along with the bass. I sat on the clay, waiting for her to look back, and when the song came to an end she did.

We rode the bus home with boxes of vegetables between our legs. Ma stared out the window while I snoozed, standing in the aisle. The lights downtown glowed way beyond the highway, and the traffic clogging Shepherd blinked in and out like fireflies.

When we'd made it back to East End, shuffling through the door, Ma had me promise that I wouldn't mention the dance.

I told her I wouldn't. She pinched my arm until I swore on it.

I told her I'd keep it to myself.

4.

My father was packing himself up from our lives. That was his master plan. He could've been discreet, if he'd wanted, but he didn't. So he wasn't. His flaunting was a choice. The audacity made it deafening.

Clothes disappeared from the laundry. CDs from the shelves. A handful of photos evaporated from the walls. Even the one I couldn't help but look at whenever it jumped in my face: this half-torn Polaroid of Javi and me in the yard.

Someone must've taken it when we first bought the restaurant. Back when you could prop us next to each other without needing a Taser. He had me on his shoulders. My heels hit his chest. Both of us are glowing, smiling like we'd won something.

Ma only shrugged when I asked her where it went. She said everything left eventually.

And I opened my mouth to say that wasn't what I meant, but I didn't. I couldn't. I just let it go.

5.

One day, Javi asked Ma if our place was haunted. And it was, in a way. By our father's other woman.

It'd nearly been a year, and even if we'd never seen her she still floated over our space, over the restaurant and the apartment. We walked and talked around her. Made room for her at the table. But Ma still asked my brother if he was the one hawking the shit disappearing around the house, and he laughed in her face. He told her garbage didn't sell.

He'd started bringing his own girls back to the restaurant. The ones I'd seen around the neighborhood—leaning on windowsills, staring out at the road, slumping through dollar marts with their mothers. Ma raised a single eyebrow toward him, and when he was home, our father only smiled. Neither of them said shit about it. It was just something that happened.

In the evenings, when the sun still had us grilling on our mattresses, Javi told me where he'd stuck it, and the noises they made when he did.

On your bed, he said, pointing above the headboard.

Right there, he said, shaking his head, chuckling.

On slow days I heard the low squcaks through the walls. You could smell my brother in the hallway for hours. Javi never walked them out, but I'd wait until they finished, watching as his guests smoothed their skirts with their palms.

Most of his girls made a beeline for the door, but a few smiled my way, and one or two actually stopped to talk. They asked how old I was. Whether I got paid for working at the restaurant. They asked about my sister, where the fuck did she go all day, and I said I never knew, that sometimes I forgot she existed. They asked if the restaurant was hiring, and did I think they could get a job, and when I asked if I'd see them again you'd think I'd cracked the funniest joke.

6.

Some days, it looked like our father'd given her up. He'd join us for dinner. He'd beat eggs in the kitchen. He'd spice the pork with Ma, cracking jokes over her head.

Mijos, he said, wiping the last of the plates, tell me about your day. Tell me what's been going on.

De veras, he said, when he saw we were low on rice. It's running because it knows your mother is going to burn it.

Stop fidgeting, he said, settling his fingers into Ma's shoulders, and they'd stand like that for hours, or maybe only a couple of minutes.

They actually looked natural. Like a thing that had developed. And Ma fought it at first, but of course she let him back in.

Still—none of us were used to having him around so often. It was this thing we all had to adapt to.

One night I asked Javi whether he was for real, whether our father was back. Or was he just bullshitting.

The building's AC had broken. We'd drag this busted box fan around the dining room depending on where customers sat. That left Javi, Jan, and I sopping wet back in our bedrooms, and the sweat stung my eyes, and our mattresses sank into shallow pools.

It means his puta's left him, said Javi, which was a big deal since he never used Spanish.

He'd brought two girls back that day, one after the other.

My sister ran into both of them on their way out. After the second girl tiptoed through the kitchen, Jan found herself in my brother's doorway. He blinked back at her, pulling up his shorts.

What, he said.

Nothing, said Jan.

That's what you are, said Jan. Less than that.

I'm sure there's a nigga waiting for you in the dumpster, said Javi.

And he'd still be cleaner than you, said Jan.

Now Javi was barely awake. I brushed my toes across a pillow on the other side of his ear. When I asked him how he thought our father'd fixed things with Ma so fast, he kicked the side of my head.

You think that matters right now?

No, I said.

You learn anything in that crackwhore school you been going to?

Yeah.

Stop crying, he said. Shut your fucking eyes.

I asked Javi what did matter. He brought his hands to his face.

Idiotas, he said. That's what you and your mother have in common.

That's how I know you're her child, he said.

Our father loved Ma for the rest of the month. He mopped up behind her. Laughed at all her shitty jokes. He rubbed the tops of her knees when the silence overwhelmed us, and I wanted to drop a plate or throw a cup or crush his toes.

But after a while, Ma turned cold again.

Her face changed. Whatever he'd shattered hadn't been completely fixed. Or maybe she wouldn't allow him to snap it again because she'd learned her lesson. So just like everything else, we watched it happen, we rolled with the punches, until one evening, after we'd set our table and closed the kitchen and settled in, our father looked at all of us, and he puffed up his chest, and he told us he was going out. Better we didn't wait up.

7.

When it was finally just Ma and me, and I wasn't cruising Midtown, or stuck in the back room washing dishes, or out in Montrose fucking boys, I'd sit on one end of the sofa, and Ma'd settle into the other, and her knees would graze the edge of my thigh as she slept through the drone of the television. The AC was fixed but sopping. Our walls were still bare. Whatever bullshit we'd been watching hummed across the room.

We filled the corners with our silence. It leaked into the hallway. If you didn't know us better you might call us content. They'd built the strip mall behind us, and the drunks' songs rang through the windows. But mostly we had silence. The kind that seals your ears.

Sometimes Ma'd jolt awake, gazing like I wasn't there.

Sometimes Ma'd tell stories. Not to me, just to herself.

He was beautiful, she'd say, and I'd mute the television. Then she wouldn't say anything else, or who she was talking about, or what she'd meant.

Other times, I'd nod off, and when I woke up she'd be reading my face.

Qué?

Nothing.

And I'd close my eyes again.

But when I opened them up, she'd still just be staring.

8.

He brought me with him once. Don't ask me why.

Javi was out whoring and Ma'd been saddled with the night rush when my father stepped halfway out the door and told me to grab the keys.

He looked just as confused as I did when I handed them over. It was the same look he gave me when he watched me in the kitchen, or when he played dumb around Ma, or after Javi'd beaten my ass. Como un pato, he'd say, shaking his head, but now there was none of that. Now my father was waiting on me.

East of 610 was clogged with commuters. It made the trip west more or less uneventful. He didn't ask how I was doing, or whether the AC was too much for my face, but after I'd started to play with the radio he stopped me at Juan Gabriel.

You like this kind of music, he asked.

I didn't. But I nodded.

Of course, he said, grinning. Your mother does too.

The block we pulled onto was cleaner than ours. It had alleys and potholes, but there were blancos too. They tinkered with their yards. Walking dogs and checking mail. Some of them sat on their porches like gardenias.

I looked at my father, like maybe he had some explanation, but he sat choking the steering wheel. Eyes on the road.

We pulled in front of this little blue stucco and stopped the car.

For a minute I thought we'd pull right back out again.

But then my father opened the door. He asked what the fuck I was waiting for.

Javi and I had figured she'd be taller than Ma. Maybe a little slimmer. Blonde, with curly hair. Javi said she probably had a condo by Reliant, and I pictured her with two boys, brothers, just like us, and a daughter out in the world, and a smile like nothing anyone'd ever seen in this life. And Javi called that stupidity but eventually we decided that was a minor detail.

I guess that's all to say that I don't know what I expected. But when she opened the door, what I felt was disappointment.

She was darker than Ma. She wasn't black. Her hair was too long. Her hips were too wide. She had this funny nose, and her arms were a little fat, and she was plain—plainer than plain, enough to leave me blinking.

But she looked comfortable. That's the word for it.

That is what distinguished her.

When my father moved to hug her, she took him with

one hand. She kept her eyes on me. She asked who I was. Before I could answer, my father called me his nephew.

He said he was babysitting. A favor to his sister.

I wanted this woman not to be a fool, or to at least ask for follow-up, but all she did was smile.

She bent and touched my cheek. Asked if I wanted anything to drink. My father looked me in the face like I better not be thirsty, so I told her I wasn't. She smiled at that too.

Her walls were bright yellow like she lived in a preschool. Candles of the Virgin were all over the place. Nothing looked too expensive, but it wasn't tacky either, and that reminded me of Ma. This was one thing that they shared.

They sat me in her living room, said they'd be back in a minute. But then an hour passed. And then another one after that.

Her shelves were cluttered: empty coffee containers, pencils, old envelopes, key chains, bills, mugs, wine bottles, and coins. Plants hung in front of the windows, swaying above fans. The wood creaked beneath me as I stepped around the living room; it was a familiar sound, but that didn't make anything better.

I found a photo by the bathroom of her when she was younger. Smiling in the arms of two other men. They could've been her brothers, but maybe they weren't, and they stood in other pictures, too: smiling in a jungle, or hunched with a group in a parking lot, or huddled over a cake in a crowd at a restaurant, and that's when I saw the one of Javi and me, the picture I'd been looking for for fuck knows how long.

I'd given up on it. It'd been missing forever. And I was just about to snatch it when I heard the door open.

The woman came out in this tank top and panties. She wasn't hiding anything. She floated right past me, filled some glasses with water, handed me one.

You look thirsty, she said. You should've said something earlier.

I thanked her, thinking she'd leave.

She settled beside me, crossing her legs.

She smelled like cinnamon. No makeup or anything else.

How is your mother? she said, and I fumbled with my tongue.

Fine.

That's good.

She thinks so, too.

I'm sure, she said, frowning.

It must be tough, she said. With you and the others.

I made a face, and she smiled.

Your sister and brother, she said.

Oh, I said.

I sipped from my glass. She watched me, smiling, growing warmer in her cheeks.

You know, your father's a funny man, she said.

Sometimes, I said.

Really, she said. He is. You'll see it when you're older.

It's just one of those things, she said. You know someone as well as you can. And then they say something that surprises you. It catches you off guard.

It's an easy thing to get used to, she said. You miss it when it's gone.

I looked at this woman, in her home, and her comfort, and I wanted to slap her. I wanted to hug her.

Then my father moaned from the bedroom, a sound I'd never heard before.

The woman set a palm on her face. Like, what could we do. She told me her house was my house. When I was thirsty, I shouldn't hesitate.

Then she grabbed the other glass. She slipped out of the living room. I heard a lock click and I didn't see her again.

When the door finally opened again, I'd fallen asleep. It was just my father. He shook me awake. He didn't say a word, but he nodded toward the car, and I patted my pocket with the photo and then we were gone.

9.

Ma was at the table when we made it back. My father stepped around her, and she didn't even blink.

Mijo, she said.

I sat at the table beside her. My father opened his mouth, but then closed it. He disappeared.

Ma asked me if I'd eaten.

I said I wasn't hungry.

Ma asked if I felt sick.

I told her I didn't.

She kept one hand on my forehead, rubbing my face with her other one, and I couldn't meet her eyes. I couldn't do that for anything.

Jan stepped out, she said.

She'll come back soon, I said.

Ma squeezed the fat on my neck.

You all make it back eventually, she said.

And we stayed that way for hours. Sitting and breathing our air. At some point, Ma told me I should probably get to bed.

And I should too, she said, but she sounded less sure.

Back in our room, Javi smoked with the window open. The breeze was the first one we'd gotten all summer. I had already tossed my shirt, and rolled onto the mattress. I willed my eyes to sleep when he sat on my head. He grinded his knuckles into my chest.

So, he said, what'd she look like?

I shut my eyes a little tighter. I asked who he meant. He sighed, like what he wanted to do was break my legs.

You know, he said. The slut.

I blinked against his thigh. My brother was getting older. Had hair creeping up his cheeks and down the sides of his ankles. A few months later, one of his girls would end up pregnant, and I'd only find out after she came around looking for him. Of course she wouldn't keep it, and he'd sulk through the house for weeks, but after that Javi was back to fucking whoever whenever.

She was beautiful, I said.

Yeah?

A real belleza. Just like you said.

No shit, said Javi. No fucking wonder.

White? he asked.

Like you said.

And her tits, said Javi. They were huge, right?

Right.

Fuck, said Javi. No wonder.

He sat on the mattress, kneading my shoulder, lost in thought. I could smell the smoke on his shirt. I tried keeping it in my lungs, but I couldn't do it. The air slipped out just like everything else.

Then Javi stood up. Grabbed his cigarettes by the window. Once he'd pulled one for himself, he waved the box at me.

I shook my head.

Pussy, he said.

10.

After we left the woman's house we didn't say much of anything, but I would not see her again and my father would not go back. I don't know where the fuck she went.

We made it out of the Heights but we didn't take the highway. My father inched the car from block to block, running every other stop sign. We drove by the bayou on White Oak and over the bridge on Westheimer, and halfway down the East End overpass I noticed he'd been staring at me.

Qué, I said.

No importa.

No. Tell me.

I knew he might smack me for talking smart. He'd turn it into a lecture on respect, or minding the ones that brought you into the world.

But he didn't do any of that. He kept his eyes on the road.

Then he let out a low whistle.

It doesn't matter, he said. Está bien.

Just remember that, he said. Either way, it's all right.

And I didn't know what that meant. And I didn't ask him either.

We took the feeder down to Wayland. We slammed the car doors in front of the house. The porch lights had been dimmed, but you could still smell the oil from the stove.

Está bien, he said, and then one more time, and then we opened the door, and we were home.

SHEPHERD

Gloria blew through our lives on a Wednesday, and our mother told us to treat her like pottery, to not ask questions, to creep around the house like ants before their queen. Our mother, who returned grape bunches over single sourings; who'd shipped my sister, Nikki, to Tech with a knife in her pillowcase; who'd slipped into this country, this home, her life, on the whim of a fortune-teller, from the eastern coast of Port Antonio, after she'd told her, peasant to peasant, that good things came to women who looked to the shore. This premonition cost her four American dollars, and if you asked my mother now you'd think she was still pissed off about it. So Gloria (thought my mother) was following a manifest destiny, universal to her people (our people), ubiquitous to her heritage (my heritage)—although she may not have said this in so many words, or even at all, if I'm honest.

We'd heard about our cousin. It was the usual family circus. We knew she was coming from Kingston, after bouncing from Mandeville to Ochi to Portmore. She'd fled to South Beach, I think, after the island became inhospitable, back when the last thing you could hope for in Miami was hospitality. She'd been a student in Jamaica, once, and then a mother, briefly, and then (most scandalously) a prostitute, one of those women who open their legs for soursop (my mother's words again). We heard she'd had a baby on the island, a little boy named Dylan, and they'd had to cut him out, which island doctors are loath to do; but then the baby died, from sepsis, or pneumonia, one of those things that occasionally happens to babies in some countries but never in others; and this, above all, was why she'd left the Caribbean for Miami, looking for work, and why she was now coming to see us in Houston; for a change of scenery, some time away, a chance to slow things down.

Our family moved, again, after my father landed the promotion. He recruited for an oil mogul downtown, and the mogul had finally struck oil. Our new place sat on Shepherd and Willowick, in the middle of River Oaks, Houston's oasis for new money, but the only differences I could pick out were the paint, the veranda, the sofas choked in shrink-wrap. Which my mother said made me ungrateful. Which she called another reason to welcome Gloria (the beloved) home—as a woman who'd been through *It,* someone who *appreciated* a rough time.

Nikki said that's all Jamaica was: a rough time. Four months at Texas Tech had made my sister sharp. Now she smoked kush with the windows open; she'd read *Les Fleurs du Mal* unabridged; she wore tight red pants and Sonic Youth tees, but never around our mother and always after dark. She fucked whiteboys from the corner store and left them in her bed. I caught one from my high school, once, checking his phone while lying on the comforter, and when he finally saw me peeking I did my best to look indifferent.

You wouldn't know a rough time if it pissed on you, said my mother, nodding toward our father, who raised an empty Shiner as he nodded toward the television. He'd been to Jamaica twice. Lanky, and graying, still broad-shouldered, even then, the second time around he made it back to the States with a wife.

Grow up and have babies, Chris, said my mother. Then you'll see.

Let one of them quit on you, she said. Then you'll see.

And she looked to me for confirmation, which I gave.

In the airport, Gloria's dress glowed a shade of margarita. Her sandals smacked. You could see the tops of her ankles as she hovered toward baggage claim. She hugged the aunt she'd heard so much about, slid into the arms of her handsome American uncle. Nikki had opted out of the airport, promising a meal when we made it back home—but, really, I knew she was roasting a bowl, yakking on the phone with one of her tricks around the block.

When Gloria reached me, she bent to squeeze my ears.

And your name is, she said, in patois thick enough to knock on.

I'd never in my life seen an actual whore (according to Nikki), a night worker (my father), or a calf in the wilderness (who else), so I looked her in the eyes for the thing that made it so; but all I saw was just some lady.

Long hair. Tall heels. Ma said she was in her thirties, but I couldn't believe it, her skin was too smooth.

I told Gloria my name was Chris and she was pretty, and she smiled like mandolins ringing.

Now that I've rolled around and had some lovers I can tell you a secret: the difference between people with the wildness in them, and people like us, is you usually can't tell until it's past too late. It's just too much a hidden part of them. Days and months and years'll pass before a person reveals themselves—and then all of a sudden they've fucked the postman, or left the gas on, or stuck their hands in your child's pants.

Nikki met us at the door. My mother told her to fetch the bags. One thing my sister hadn't forgotten in Lubbock was the kitchen—how to bring a grouper back to life on the stove—and we smelled the ocean from the driveway, and we moved a little quicker for it. She nodded at Gloria on her way out, and it was a look I'd grown acquainted with: I Will Tolerate You Out of Necessity, and Not a Second Longer Than Required. But what Gloria did was grab her wrist.

She looked her in the nose.

You have, said Gloria, the most beautiful eyes.

It was the first time in years that I'd heard Nikki stammer. She thanked her cousin. She said she was tired. There'd been loads to cook, a house to clean, preparations to make, et cetera, but even if we couldn't smell her stash from the driveway, I saw it in the curve of Gloria's lips.

Funny, said Gloria. Must be rough being a student.

When she finally let her go, my sister actually exhaled.

We ate at the table. The kitchen, like the rest of the house, was what our father called a "work in progress," with the walls all moon yellow and spice pink and lime green, weighed down by Matisse and Tintoretto and El Greco prints. Paintings were my parents' thing—a new one materialized every few months.

Gloria stopped in front of the Greco—the one where Christ's holding the cross, eyes peeled back like he's taking a piss—and when she asked my father if he'd seen the original, he stared, for a solid second, waiting for the punch line.

It didn't come.

He said he hadn't.

It's beautiful, said Gloria, almost as pretty as the Ugolino da Siena.

His eyes were still bugging when my mother reached the table; and Gloria lit up. She said the one thing she hadn't expected from Nikki was a plateful of plantain. My mother couldn't have glowed any brighter, because we'd been eating the damn dish my whole life, it was one of her childhood staples, she'd forced Nikki to learn the recipe back when my sister still gave a shit and not one of us had ever spoken in favor of it (if anything, it made us sick).

Yes, she said, smiling. We were away from the island in body, but never in heart. Certainly not for dinner.

Gloria nodded, and my father smirked, and Nikki glowered from her corner of the table.

She asked to be excused. Our mother laughed a single Ha.

Rudeness, she said, the girl leaves for school like a princess and comes back a pig; and Nikki barked at that, she said it wasn't like she was the only one; and it was almost the start of another Household Uprising, until Gloria coughed, and smiled, and explained that she, too, had been Punk.

Besides, said Gloria, life is long. Let your daughter live while she can.

Standing slowly, my cousin gripped the table, for support, and then, apropos of nothing, or maybe in rebellion of it, Gloria, mouth full of grouper, kissed my father on his lips.

I remember my father puckering.

And I remember my mother's face.

And Gloria waved to the rest of us, starting her long limp upstairs.

And we sat unspeaking, with the refrigerator's hum in the foreground, until Nikki reared back, slowly, and laughed.

Gloria grew up in Kingston, and lived there until she couldn't, until it became something like a war zone, before it turned into what it is now. Her parents passed for intellectuals on the island—teaching literature at UWI—and my cousin grew up on wood floors, with Ravel and Mahler conducting the apartment. She took her first steps on paperbacks lining the rugs—on the face of Javier Marías, on the back of Derek Walcott—and even as Jamaica's knees began to buckle, under narcotics, under voodoo politics, and the sidewalks began to choke with the homeless, the drugged, and the cracked out, her parents held her close, filled her ears with what comfort they could. She grew up loved. She never forgot that.

But, eventually, her folks got caught up too. Slowly at first. And then all of a sudden. The money for the coke came from money for their clothes, and then the money for their bills, and then the money for their apartment.

Later on, Gloria told me she hadn't been upset but even strolling down the corner for books became a burden, a needless risk. Kingston had begun to swallow itself. She was risking her life for poems. And she felt herself sinking, whether or not she was in the house, parents prone on the floor, noses crusty from yesterday's binge.

Even still, they had to eat. So Gloria became the breadwinner. She was fifteen, with nothing like a marketable skill, but there are always ways to make some bank in the Caribbean if you're young and beautiful and willing.

She knew some girls who worked the resorts. They knew some girls who weren't opposed to another player.

Gloria started working the cruise ports. Businessmen and bachelors and newlyweds, mostly, but occasionally she'd find herself an islander, a big man with a little extra cash, and these were the ones she passed on to the next girl, because they reminded her of something she didn't want to think about. But, despite everything, she found time to read—she spent some of the money she was saving for a lifeline on books. She hit the resorts; she discovered Milton; she worked the coast; she discovered Rimbaud; she bought some heels; she discovered Babel; she took care of her skin; she discovered Rumi; she tried not to catch the clap; she discovered Borges; she caught the clap; she discovered Allende; she waited it out; she discovered

Plath; she tried not to catch anything else. There'd been a baby named Dylan, she'd named him after the poet; but one day Dylan died, and of course she couldn't find the father. She couldn't even have guessed what he looked like.

Our mother didn't retaliate after the kiss. This confused me. It disrupted a logical sequence of events. I remember when she spat on the grocer in Sharpstown, because he'd refused to accept an expired coupon for bananas. I remember when my father failed to replace the bedroom's air filters, and she'd stuffed them in herself, and he'd had to phone a repairman. I remember when Nikki first left for college, after the crying and the hugging and the promise of weekly visits; and how, after she hadn't called, for the second Sunday in a row, my mother rode the nine-hour bus to Lubbock to ask what, specifically, was the problem. But on that evening, and every other night for the next few months, all she did was grin.

Gloria's still smelling the sand, she said.

I was wild when I was her age too, she said.

All it takes is a little time, she said; but my father stayed out of Gloria's way—he'd shiver a little when she slipped into the room.

But Gloria's presence wasn't a burden. My cousin was supposed to be kicking her feet up—that was the point of her stay. And since she didn't ask for much at all, sometimes I even forgot about her. She slept in the guest room, although my mattress was what she'd been promised, but she never called me out on it. Gloria said it didn't matter. She could fit just about anywhere. And Nikki didn't doubt it; she said that vermin would always adapt.

In fact, Gloria said, I should sleep at the foot of her bed, or I should at least bring in a sleeping bag, that she wouldn't mind the company.

My father was skeptical. He simply frowned when she suggested this. But my mother called it a Good Idea: I could act as a runner, could keep Gloria off her feet.

So I shook the cobwebs off some blankets from the attic, and after my first night on the floor Gloria told me she didn't need a runner, or assistance, or whatever, because she just wanted company. She needed someone else to talk to, it made her think less of her son.

Going into the summer, I'd had my own plans: we'd entered that part of July where the days begin to swallow themselves. The houses in our neighborhood fit together like box tops, with their pastel reds and blues and whites, and I rode bikes with Anwar Baz and Jeff Tan and Kyle Okri, blazing past porch stoops manned by the daughters we deified. Every once in a while, one of us got bold, asking if they had any ice water inside. We'd already talked about making it past the porch. What we'd do if they let us in, if they asked us to pull it out. This was the summer we were going to get laid, to touch and to suck and to fuck, if they let us. Eventually Anwar snagged some condoms from his brother, but of course we had nowhere to put them. We tried our hand at a dime of weed (courtesy of Jeff's older sisters downtown) but I spent that evening lost inside of myself, marveling at all of the space in my head no one had taken the time to tell me about.

With my father negotiating vendors downtown, and my mother scouring the foreclosures for bargains, we mostly had the house to ourselves. Nikki and Gloria struck up a truce: if one shared her books, then the other would shut her mouth. Nikki holed up in her room with Bobby from the supermarket, and Rafa from the gas station, and Jacob from the pool. And despite clear instructions from her island doctor to stay in one place, to stop moving so goddam much, Gloria found ways to get out and about, from the porch, to the living room, to the sidewalks lining the cul-de-sac. No one knew she was gone until she finally came back.

Some days Gloria told me stories. She told me about the red-light district in Kingston. About the palms in Ocho Rios, which bent inwards like arches. About how roads sank in the hill country, how she'd found jewelry in the mud. She told me about trips to London, to São Paulo, to New York, and how the World Trade Center memorial had made her feel mortal, like she didn't matter at all. She told me about beaches in Antigua where babies drank the water. About the seagulls in Haiti, how she'd fed them, how they'd thanked her.

In the mornings, she brewed coffee and read. It was the only time that she glowed. She'd start with my father's *Business Affairs,* and my mother's outdated *Oprah*s; after lunch, she'd slip into Nikki's shelves, with the Bolaño and the Woolf and the Calvino and the Foucault. She flipped through Chekhov. She nosed through Tanikawa. She threw a long-lost copy of *Huck Finn* at the wall.

Gloria asked me for highlighters and underlined everything. She read beautifully, deeply. I don't know how else to describe it.

Eventually, I finally asked her what she got out of reading these books by old dead men, what the words on the page had to do with her. The kind of question an idiot asks. But she took it seriously, she pursed her lips.

It's just another way to talk to the dead, she said.

It's another way to make a way, she said.

She finally brought up Dylan on a walk. Okri had skittered away on his bike, down the road and into the skyline, because Anwar and Jeff had made it past the porch, but not us. We hadn't seen much of them lately. Gloria asked me who Okri was, and I called him a friend, my friend, and Gloria smiled, nodding, and in a tone of voice that I will never forget she insisted that she understood, even if I didn't yet, and then she squeezed my knuckles.

Dylan was underweight, she explained, but the doctor told me he'd grow.

Light like you (and here she prodded my stomach), or maybe more like your father.

Like his dad, I asked, and she agreed, but more like me.

His fingers were this big, she said.

I pushed my thumb through the circle she'd made, pointing toward the road and the city it led to.

The nurse said he cried too much, she said, but really he was laughing. That's it. All he ever did was laugh.

I told her she could have another baby, and she frowned—the first one I'd ever actually seen on her face. She said it probably wouldn't happen. She said her body couldn't take it (or maybe that *she* couldn't take it, I thought).

I knew I'd lost her, so I tried to backtrack: I said her son would've been a real man, the kind I would've looked up to, and Gloria said, Yes, he would've been, and I knew that I'd done something Good.

July was on its way out when my father got the second raise. The mogul had struck gold, again, and his profits trickled down to the lowest rung. We braced ourselves for another move but my father said no, what we ought to do was wait; the neighborhood was nice, or at least nice enough. Besides, we had a houseguest, supposedly on bed rest, and what were we as a family if not considerate of others? My mother made vague noises of taking a trip, swooping through Jamaica for the first time in years, but these were just words. We knew that they wouldn't actually go. She hadn't touched its soil since she'd taken off from the tarmac.

One day, Okri and I spent an afternoon in the bayou. We walked the length of the neighborhood to reach it, until we crossed the freeway, where we had to wade through the muck in our sneakers. He suggested we take our shoes off, because of course they were getting filthy, the water was full of shit, and then we were stepping through it, soaking the rest of our clothes. We were sopping, really; so slowly, categorically, we began to strip: first our pants, as we stepped through the stream, then our shirts, once we'd found ourselves tangled in vines, until we were wading through the water in our shorts, with the highway above us, where we reached a clearing beneath an overpass. And Okri and I laughed, just at the sight of each other. Our clothes were irreparable. We smelled like shit. And we decided, or we came to the conclusion, that we should grope one another, tenderly, and then furiously; and we did this, wordlessly, touching without kissing; and when he'd finished, and I'd finished, he made a joke about the cars going by above us, something banal, but necessary if we were to survive the walk back.

And that's what we did. We picked up our shit and we walked back.

We made it home to the neighborhood, and we slipped into sneakers, and we never talked about it then, or since.

I spent the next few days in a funk. My mood was indistinguishable to my parents (I was already pretty quiet most days; compounding that silence meant nothing whatsoever) and Nikki didn't care much one way or the other. One morning, eating an egg sandwich at the table, I began to shake, my toes first, my legs, until the chills made their way to my fingers, and Nikki watched me from the counter, said I'd never get any ass if I stayed so fucking weird.

Gloria noticed. She was starting to get better. She'd mentioned buying her return ticket soon. She'd make a go of it back on the island, she said, it was time to start planning ahead; but my mother told her not to think anything of it—she really wasn't a burden. When Gloria asked me what was wrong, I told her nothing, nothing at all, but in a way that implied that everything was, in fact, very wrong, that the most wrong thing had occurred, that wrong had become my reality.

A few evenings later, I knew what I had to do. Gloria and I slept in the guest room, on the other side of the house from my parents. She slept late and she read, and sometimes she told stories, and other times she just cried herself to sleep, but on this particular night I asked her to tell me about her work. She looked at me as if I were joking, or maybe it was because she hoped I was joking, but I wasn't. I wasn't. I told her I wanted to know.

She said she wasn't sure if she knew what I was asking. I really should go back to bed.

I said that my mother had called her a whore. A prostitute. A soursop woman.

That if what my mother said was true, then the least she could do was prove it.

We wore the same look on our faces, one of disbelief; that these words were even forming in my mind, that they were leaving my mouth, that they were in the air between us, the air we'd come to think of as our own, shared.

But it wasn't, and they were, and I kept talking. I said terrible things.

I said the books and the trinkets and the family—my family—that she thought were her escape were no escape at all.

I said she felt like she had to escape because she had no escape.

I said her son was better off without her, that she was better off without a son.

When I'd finished Gloria asked me if that was all. If

it was, she said, then she was tired. She'd like to go to sleep. She said I should go to my room, my real room, and when I stood up to leave she said to shut the door behind me.

From that evening on, I was ashamed.

I no longer slept on the floor. I left every room that Gloria entered, sat silently at our table. My mother slapped me, once, for ignoring my cousin at dinner, and my father asked, twice, if anything was wrong (I don't remember my response). Nikki didn't broach my behavior, because I wasn't Nikki's problem, and even when I'd considered clueing her in I ended up changing my mind.

And then, one evening, Gloria slipped into my room. I wasn't sure what time it was, it could've been one or four, one of those hours when it no longer makes a difference. She asked me what was wrong, and I didn't reply. She asked me again what was wrong, and I pretended to snore. She asked me what was wrong, and she touched my shoulder, and I told her I was broken. She asked me what that meant, and I didn't say a word, I opened my eyes and looked right at her, or I looked right past her, because I couldn't see anything at all.

We sat there in silence; as Gloria held my shoulder and I looked past her, and then she told me that she understood. Or that she didn't understand, not really, but she understood enough.

She placed her hand on my knee, and I watched it sit there, not moving, until it began to rise, until it reached my thigh, and then it rose higher, until Gloria was touching my cheek, and she was looking at my face, and then we were kissing, and then it was both of her hands, and we looked through each other, deeply, because she was no longer on the edge of the mattress, she'd maneuvered herself on top of me, she'd slipped some of me inside of her, and Gloria told me to look up, to look into her eyes, and I couldn't do it, it wouldn't work, I started crying, my god, until she finally set her ear on my shoulder and told me everything would be fine, everything would be okay, it would all turn out okay.

About a month later, Gloria flew back to Kingston. Nikki didn't see her off this time either. My sister was packing for her own return, and she gave Gloria the roughest of nods, and my cousin wished her well in all of her future endeavors. I didn't show my face—I told everyone I was sick. My mother told me this didn't matter, I didn't know when I'd see Gloria again and I needed to come out right now and say goodbye, but my father said to leave me alone, it wouldn't make anything better, and besides, I only felt that way because I loved her. This, he said, was obvious.

I remember watching Gloria step into the van from the driveway, and she waved from inside the car, and eventually I waved back. She'd left a book for me on her bed; she'd written something in it, she told me I'd know when to read it. But I didn't read it then. And then the book was lost. And I left home, and I came back, and when it was finally time or when I thought it was finally time, it wasn't there to open, and whatever she'd written had disappeared. I asked my mother where she'd put that book, where the fuck it could've gone, and she said there were so many books in the house she had no way of knowing for sure. She told me to calm down. It couldn't have been that important.

WAYSIDE

1.

Javi and his boy Rick sold smoke on the court. This was after our father left, and our sister moved out, but before my brother enlisted. They usually pulled just enough to make it worth their while, and their clientele were the usual suspects—güeros toking up after class, suits stocking up for the weekend. But every once in a while their plug would spot them extra weight, whatever kush he hadn't already passed off, and it was just enough for Javi to bring back to Ma's kitchen.

Our patrons knew the score. They knew Ma ran the place on fumes. We were always short on rent, always out of everything on the menu. Even if the patrons were my father's friends, they knew he'd bailed on them too.

They paid Javi the street price. It got us from month to month. And it worked until Ma finally caught him dealing at the register.

She kept cool in the moment. She let him get his money. But that night she popped him, spitting all of her Spanish at once.

Javi countered that it was all for a higher cause—we'd start a little savings, enough to fix the place up. Maybe coat some paint on the walls, buy her a couple of dresses, kick a little extra pay to the cooks that still showed up. But Ma only said if he kept fucking around he could pack his shit and follow his dad.

Idiota, said Ma. Dumber than a dog.

If you need money, said Ma, you ask me.

Right, said Javi, and you'll just grab it from the bank.

We'll stay open a little longer. We'll figure it out. I'll talk to Jan.

Do that, said Javi. Let me know when you find her.

Rick laughed when I told him a few days later. He ruffled my hair, said life really wasn't that hard.

He was cool with Ma. He looked her in the eye. Rick was taller than Javi, the most light-skinned out of all of us, and he carried himself like all of kindness in a bottle.

He told Javi it didn't matter—he'd spot us some cash on his own. No reason to have the señora strung out over bullshit.

But Javi told him to chill. He said Rick wasn't family.

That's what it is to be a man, said Javi. Entiendes? You do what the fuck you have to for your own.

And Rick just put his hand on my shoulder, shaking his head like, Whatever.

He wasn't really a hood but people still saw him around. Rick lived a block off Wayside, with his aunts and this girl he was fucking. He was always on the verge of getting out of the drug thing—someday a door would open and he'd swoop right out of that life—but Javi told me how, once, someone'd gotten too familiar, and Rick broke the dude's jaw with his own ten fingers.

Except it's one of those stories I can never believe. Rick scored me shakes off the dollar menu. Brought me tamales wrapped by his tías. He taught me how to whistle, cut my splinters out with his switchblade, and he never got on me about being a dumbass.

Once, on a slow day, Javi called him a pato. A know-nothing faggot. We were watching business from a park bench. Sometimes they hit that square with the playground on Palmer and Sherman, for the moms, and Rick was waving his hands at some whitelady like he'd just finished trimming her shrubs.

I told Javi to take it back. I told him to shut his mouth.

My brother got all wide-eyed like he was about to beat my ass. But he didn't. He just said I didn't know anything at all.

Pero yo sé un maricón cuando lo veo, he said. Yo sé.

And you will too, he said. Just watch.

2.

Meanwhile—back at home, cash at the restaurant was still tight. Ma even laid off a little about the pot.

Then one of Javi's deals went wrong and some boys knocked him up with a bat. He was mouthing off, doing his Javi thing, and they simply hadn't felt like hearing it. He was off the court for a month. Had everyone on the block calling him Creed.

Which put us in a bind. He and Rick had a good thing

going, but no way could one handle their weight without the other. And Rick said not to worry, he told Javi he'd ask around for a sub, but my brother called that unacceptable. He told Rick it wasn't his place.

I'll manage, said Javi.

Bullshit, said Rick.

Watch me.

So you'd really rather run your brother out of a house on some pride shit?

Watch your mouth, cabrón. You don't even fucking know.

I know you're being a fool, said Rick.

And Javi opened his mouth, but then he closed it right back up.

I don't actually remember how I suggested I should deal—just the silence between them when I brought it up, and Javi's laughter afterwards. Rick had this look like a bulb about to burst. I said it'd be easier that way.

Their buyers knew my face. I'd watched them score for years. Rick and Javi's only other option was to bring someone else in, someone off the court, which wasn't about to happen.

We were sprawled on the stoop lining Rick's front porch. My brother's cheeks had popped, swollen, blushing like a pair of bruised peaches. He chewed on his lip, frowning out at the road, and when a voice called for Rick from inside the house, he nudged the door shut with his toe.

Javi called it plausible. He'd heard shittier ideas. Rick called it fucked that we were considering it at all.

If he wants to drop his huevitos, I say we let him,

said Javi. He's been mooching long enough. It's about fucking time.

Rick told him he was bugging, he said it wasn't right, and Javi sat up and he spat and said the only one tripping was Rick.

3.

So the next week I was out there. The afternoon was chilly. Rick loaned me a hoodie, this red thing torn at the elbows. The court wasn't packed, just the usual still life in motion: grownass niggas macking on girls, stiffs hooping on the rims. Rick got most of the traffic, he touched all of the hands, but every now and again someone shuffled over to me.

I was Javi for the day. Spoke with my hands unless I was spoken to. One guy just shook his head when he saw me, like wasn't I still a baby, and I said if he wanted to get his fix it was none of his fucking business.

By the end of the day we'd pulled the money for rent, and a little for the next month too. That night, the two of them stole me a 40, carrying me drunk across Leeland, weaving through the cars parked by the stadium. I wasn't the kid who drank, that was the one vice I'd dodged, but with Rick's hands on my waist I couldn't help but wonder why it'd taken me so long.

Javi said I had huevos. A fucking man's huevos now. Rick just laughed at that, swinging me higher.

My legs wouldn't work. I couldn't tell right from down. But none of that shit mattered. I couldn't stop smiling.

It's the baby face, said Javi. It brought all the bitches in.

He's a natural, said Rick, but not like it was a good thing.

When my brother slipped inside the CVS for a six-pack, Rick and I stooped by the dumpsters facing Polk. Traffic had started its descent downtown. Between the catcalls on the road, and the bass thumping from I-45, Rick gave me a squeeze before he spat on the concrete.

Nice job today.

Thanks, I said.

You needed this, he said. Now you know what it's like.

I already knew.

But now you really know.

I didn't see what that meant. I was too fucked to care. I smiled at Rick, chipped a fist across his shoulder.

But he shrugged it off. He spat again.

I asked him what was up, what the hell was his problem, and when Rick bent down I felt his breath on my earlobes.

It felt like electricity. Like somebody'd gone and woken me up.

He said I was better than this. I should be better than this.

But you have to do it yourself, he said. These fuckers won't do it for you.

Javi slumped out with the beer, shouting something about screwing the cashier. He grabbed Rick's shoulder, and Rick gave Javi's a squeeze.

Something important had happened. Something had changed. But I didn't know what, so I tore a can from the plastic.

4.

A couple months later Rick was blown up on the court. Shots all over his face and his arms and his back. I wasn't there, I can't tell you for sure, but I heard he'd been making the last of his rounds.

When I told Javi that was it for me, that I wouldn't be dealing again, he actually laughed in my face. He asked if I'd honestly thought he'd been holding out for it.

We ended up passing through the wake. Ma came too, in this dress that was way too much for mourning. She talked up Rick's mother while we stood in the back, with all of the aunts and a girl laced in black. She had hazel eyes, with this crazy look on her face, and when they finally opened the casket she wailed like a parrot.

When we made it to the body, my brother snatched my hand. He made me touch Rick's face. He told me this was what happened to fags.

A few months later Rick was blown up on the count[illegible]
[illegible] all over [illegible] his arms and [illegible] wasn't
[illegible]
[illegible]

[illegible]
[illegible]
[illegible] nothing.

We started passing through the shade [illegible] the two
months since that was too much for mourning. She
held up Rick's mother while we stood in the back, with
all of the [illegible] and [illegible] dressed in black. She had her
[illegible] on her face, and when they [illegible]
[illegible] the wake like a parrot.

When we had left the body, my brother [illegible] my
hand. [illegible] Rick's [illegible] He told me this was
what happened to [illegible]

BAYOU

Mix found his chupacabra next to the bayou, under the bridge, and by the time he ran to fetch me it'd bled in the water and died.

For better or worse, this wasn't the worst thing that'd happened. Mix and I were broke. We'd flunked out of the community college. My girl, Denise, was having someone else's baby, and I'd been living down by Shepherd, out in the Heights, back with Gran. Her place sat behind what were basically cardboard houses, leaning against the wind like a baby'd scribbled them in, and Gran had started slipping Navy pamphlets under my door, which Mix called unfortunate, and debilitating, but hilarious—like, picture my fat ass in somebody's uniform, because you couldn't even do it without the buttons pegging your nose.

That these things could keep happening and life could keep going was more mysterious to me than whatever the fuck he was showing me.

It was also hot as shit. Typical Houston.

The chupacabra was hairless and brown. Pale under the

paws. I looked at the body with the gnats creeping around it, and then at Mix, and then the chupacabra again, and I thought about whether the stench was rigor mortis or just the sunburnt factories across the 10.

Mix said it might be a dog or something but obviously it was not. I knew dogs. We had bitches all over the block. The North Side was where they came to die, between the alleys and the laundromats lining the feeder.

This thing had fat fangs. Crooked ears. Stripes on its back.

And it looked a little spooked.

Like it'd made some big mistake.

Like it'd been looking for something better but it'd ended up with us.

An hour later, it coughed.

Fuck, said Mix.

He was barefoot and he poked it with a hairy toe, and the torso sort of deflated, and its chest began to rise and sink and rise and sink again.

Mix reached for my phone. I told him I had to jet.

You have to work, he said. I give you the gift of modern mystery, and you dodge it to sweep for gabachos?

Gabachos tip better than everyone else.

You've got no class, he said. No vision.

No plata, I said. No choice.

Hijo de puta, said Mix, motherfuckers always got a choice, and he popped a squat with my cell, and he snapped like twelve photos. The flash had both of us wincing.

Mix was short for Mixcoatl. Which I'd never heard him pronounce. The one place you saw it was his name tag for the Sushi Shack, where we both worked. He only wore the fucking thing because no one could say it, and if no one could say it then no one could ask him to do anything. He'd stand at the counter for hours, handing back incorrect change. Dipping his fingers in everyone's rice and sighing at all of our customers.

T, he said, this is our big break. We make ourselves viral with this thing right here.

He stepped around the chupacabra, holding the phone and snapping photo after photo. He lifted its legs, flipped the body on its side. The chupacabra wheezed a little, jerking its ears, and Mix threw back his hand. But it only began to snore.

We unclenched. Exhaled.

If it wakes up with a paycheck I'll stay, I said.

You don't get it, said Mix.

Let's say we break even with this, said Mix. Let's say we go big.

You go ahead and hold your breath.

I'm keeping your phone, said Mix.

When I asked him why, he told me to jump-start my brain.

To call the fucking *Chronicle,* he said. The fucking mayor. Fucking KUHF and the six o'clock news.

Monsters in Alief, he said. You can't make that shit up.

But you probably could, I said.

And it's probably a raccoon, I said.

Go off and play kitchen, said Mix. He was already dialing.

Go play the other man, he said. Earn some pennies for your bastard.

You fuck all the way off with that.

It's not like you don't already know.

And I started to say that knowing something didn't give you license to shout it—like how I knew Mix was a fag, but it wasn't something we talked about—but then the chupacabra opened its eyes. And the two of us jumped. And then Mix fell on his ass, and I was right behind him.

It looked up at the both of us.

We froze. Held our breath.

It had talons like glossed talc. They tore at the grass. And it shivered, sort of, as if the heat weren't shit to it at all. The chupacabra could've been hungry, or thirsty, or lost, or maybe all of those things, or maybe none of them at all, and I looked at Mix to tell him, like, we should totally leave it alone, its crew would come back for it, but then Mix caught my eye, and he lifted a single finger, and he was on the phone popping off about what a fucking discovery we'd made.

Like I said—we worked at the Sushi Shack. You got your fish blinking on these trays like right in front of you. The chefs had these tattoos the size of your foot, with the faces of their wives, or at least that's what they told us, and they'd gripe about you handling the trays without mitts but then the mitts went missing and we'd find them in their cubbies.

Right before I punched out, I thought about calling Denise. But then I remembered Mix. Who'd kept my cell. And the thing he'd needed it for.

So I wiped the tatami. Washed the rice. Scrubbed the piss from the toilets, greeted the moms drunk off lukewarm sake. I watched high schoolers push silverware onto the carpet, snapping their fingers for a server until I stooped to pick it up, and when I asked Tanaka-sama if it was cool to use the landline, she nodded wordlessly, frowning, stoic.

She'd been nodding since Mix'd introduced us. She'd nodded when I'd asked how to tell when the salmon turned. She'd nodded, months back, when I'd poked her for a raise, and when I finally got my check she'd actually shaved a little off. She claimed it was for all of the food I'd stolen—she understood, it's just how my people were—which I denied, obviously, because I hadn't, at least not yet; but that was my cue. From then on, I was the fucking Hamburglar.

I'd wrap the salmon and the tuna and the rice in plastic. Walked all four courses right back home to Gran. And she'd ask why I'd gone and brought a goddam fish tank, why I couldn't have found a casserole dish like everyone else.

Straight out the ocean, she said. They don't even wash it.

Oldest people in the world and they got no good sense, she said.

I tried ringing Denise.

Of course she didn't answer.

So I walked my ass home. Gran wasn't around. Most nights, she was channeling Moses in some pulpit. I wedged the door behind me, reached through the sofa cushions for the phone card, but all I found were the Bibles and the fans and the *Jets*.

Her place has two rooms if you don't count the bathroom. If you do, then we have two and half of a quarter. Neither of us can use it without the other dialing in, which makes nature and its precedents inexpressible, unimaginable.

Gran was allegedly born in the backyard. Her daughter, my mother, was born in the bedroom. I left the womb in the Emergen-C off the feeder road, but Gran tells everyone I was spawned here too. It makes a better parable than her daughter's drunken delivery, and the cigarettes they'd taken from her purse like right afterwards.

My mother's love story was the usual hood dramedy: first she met a boy, some southside Breno Mello. Gran'd warned her that the locals were nothing but trouble, but her tolerance only went so far. She wasn't down with mixing. And her daughter heeded that, at first, like a good Baptist girl, but my father just kept shaking his hips out in East End, dancing bachata up and down Westheimer, blowing kisses at her face, doing that thing with his tongue, and eventually she gave in like anyone else.

He knocked her up in the usual way. For six minutes it looked like he'd stick around.

But then I was born, and he stepped out for a glass of water, and believe it or not he's been thirsty ever since.

I'm told my mother held me close. That she'd smiled. Pinched my cheeks. And after the usual recovery riffraff, she took off to find her guy.

They never got hitched. But of course he'd taken her to prom. Gran still keeps the photo before the dance on the mantel. They're smiling, draped in formal wear and looking suspiciously close to happy, and most days if I remember I'll stuff the frame behind the candles.

Gran props it right back up whenever she makes it home from church.

In our own silent way, it's how we've learned to coexist.

The phone card was in the kitchen this time, in a drawer, wedged between some forks.

I rang my cell.

Mix answered.

Hey, gordito, he said.

You reach the BBC yet?

Even better, he said. Get your fat ass over here.

I asked if the thing'd woken up. Had it made any moves.

Ándale, he said, and then he hung up.

Before I bounced, I caught Denise on the fourth ring.

TeDarus, she said, and that felt good. Her just saying it.

She studied at the college downtown. Wanted to plan the insides of buildings. It took her a year to tell me, and at first they were just words because when people here say they're doing something it's either tomorrow or the day after.

But she did it. She figured it out. And from then on, she was busy. Whenever I actually saw her I thought she'd already upped and moved.

So when she called about the baby, I didn't know who I felt worse for: the kid for coming now, at this point in time, or her for being stuck with it.

Or me for wanting it.

I realize how that makes me sound.

I asked her how she felt. Had our little parasite kicked.

Good, she said.

I asked if there was milk in the fridge, and Denise said she'd check in a bit.

I asked if there was gas in her tank, and Denise said she'd just filled up.

I asked if she wanted to chill, and Denise told me she was fine, and I clinched my ears for anything else in the background—muffled laughter, BET in the next room.

But she asked if I'd called for a reason, or was I simply fucking around, and I sort of blanked for a second. The sense just whooshed right out of my head.

I told her I was busy.

Going to an interview, actually.

When she didn't ask for what, I said it was for a project.

This thing I'd been working on.

I had found something amazing.

Something the press wanted to talk to me about.

She didn't answer for so long that I figured she'd hung up.

Then she did this little cough thing.

She said that was interesting. It was the word's first appearance between us in months, if not ever.

No doubt, I said.

They thought so too, I said.

I told her it'd been a tough sell, but stations were showing some interest. I told her I'd be on the news. I told her I'd let her know.

And Denise said, For sure, you do that, looking forward to it.

And I waited for her to say something else.

But that's when the dial tone really came.

Mix was still on my phone when I stepped through the door. He pointed at the chupacabra on his table, mouthing, Hey, pendejo.

He lived in this complex across from the Kroger. Maybe an hour's walk from Denise's. His place was always unlocked. He'd been staying there since the Great Thanksgiving Rupture, back when his brother'd found the dick pic in his pillowcase.

Now he was pacing the floor of his room. The chupacabra was wrapped in some towels under a lamp. It blinked at the two of us.

It looked like a kolache. A too-big beanie covered its ears. I reached out to touch it, and my fingers grazed the skin.

The chupacabra blinked. Shrugged my hand away. Mix'd wrapped a bandage around its paws, and another around its belly to keep it warm.

Yeah yeah yeah, said Mix, picking at a toenail.

By the highway, he said. Like, we almost ran it down.

No, he said, we didn't. But close. Pulled over and chased it.

I know, right, he said. You're so right. We totally should've.

But, he said, but! We didn't. And it made this noise! Like, aaiiee! Aaiiee! Like a cat, you know?

Not *a* cat, he said.

Like one, he said.

Yes, he said.

Claro, he said.

And then it died, he said. But now we're pretty sure it's back.

Then there was silence.

A marathon of nodding.

He read off his address. Slapped his palms together, bowed, and pantomimed a thank-you.

After another pause he tossed my cell across the room, and the chupacabra jumped when it skidded across his mattress, bouncing onto the floor.

Fuck, I said.

Shit yeah, said Mix. We've got press.

We high-fived.

I asked what that entailed, specifically.

It means we've got to get this fucker going, he said. It's got to put on a show. We've got to give it some pills or something.

Chupacabra pills, I said.

So that's what we're calling it now.

You're the one who wanted a goblin.

You know what the fuck I mean, said Mix. We're agreeing that this is a thing?

I looked at the chupacabra. It'd stuck its nose into some AUX cables. The only thing I knew was that this thing had been abandoned.

We're not agreeing on shit, I said.

And anyways, I said, you told them it was fine.

This shit looks fine to you?

That's what you said on the phone.

Pinche tonto, he said, waving me away. I said that to get them *out* here. Nobody comes through Alief just to look at a dead thing.

But it isn't dead anymore, I said, and Mix told me I was missing the point.

We've got a few hours before they show, he said. Maybe it'll start dancing or some shit. Maybe it'll get hungry.

Just in time to eat us, I said. Sounds like a plan.

And I thought he'd crack on me about my weight, or Denise, or my excuse for a fucking life, but Mix'd already stepped into the bathroom, humming, taking a leak.

We'd met like a decade earlier and even that isn't very remarkable. Maybe I was nine. He'd have been ten. Gran had me in the grocery store when Mix's mother walked up, asking if we knew where in the hell they kept the Goya.

Blanquitos, she'd said. Even their stores don't make any sense.

I was bigger than him—I was bigger than everyone—and he stood behind the shopping cart wringing his shirt.

He asked for my name.

He hasn't shut his mouth since.

Mix'd always been into monsters. Always into the unreal. He kept this gorgon print on his wall, right when you stepped through the room. His father got it for him maybe a year before he bounced, and now Mix's bed was surrounded by orcs and dragons and the leech-looking fucker from *Dune*. I never understood that shit, it never once clicked for me, but that wasn't a deal-breaker. I dealt with it. It was the least I could do.

There's the time Mix's ma got sick, and Gran had him and his brother over for dinner, and Mix vomited the okra she'd been stewing onto the good table linen.

There's the day the firecracker exploded in my hands, and Mix blew on my palms until we found some ice.

There's the day Mix told me he might like boys, and I said it didn't matter, he'd still be fuckless his whole life.

There's the day I told him I might love Denise, and he told me that I loved how she was willing to screw me.

And there's the night after graduation, when I should've been cross-faded, at some party with my girl, who'd already caught a little escape velocity, and Mix should've been at his mother's, for one of the last dinners they'd share; but actually we'd driven, on no notice, all the way up to Austin, to celebrate what we'd been told was a new chapter in our shit.

We ran out of gas halfway. It was already after midnight. Some random nigga and a vato weren't about to flag anyone down. So we slept in the bed of his brother's pickup, drenched from the humidity, wondering if anyone in this whole shitty country could be as lucky as us.

I wasn't especially proud of myself for stealing the chupacabra.

Mix'd fallen asleep. Channel 8 had called him back, left a message on my phone. The intern or whatever said they'd see us around ten.

I unwrapped the chupacabra and tucked it into Mix's gym bag. It yawned a little, exposing some fang. It looked me in the eyes, squinting, and I tried to keep its gaze.

It frowned. I zipped the bag.

This time she answered on the second ring.

Wow, I said.

T, said Denise. It's late.

I know. I wanted to show you something.

It couldn't wait, she asked, and I saw the face she'd be making, with her palm on her chin and her lips tucked in.

I've got work tomorrow, T.

It'll be quick, I said.

But you can't just tell me now?

I'd rather not.

Why?

It's a little weird.

T, she said.

You know how things are now, she said.

We've talked about this, she said, and that's when I told her I knew that, that I was aware, that if she listened for two fucking minutes she'd see.

There was silence on the line.

I wanted to eat my tongue.

I'd never raised my voice at Denise. I didn't know it was something I could do. But a part of me knew however she replied would determine the next decade of my life.

Well, she said. I'm up.

You know the code for the gate, she said.

And TeDarus, she said, don't you ever in your life do that again.

Denise lived in one of those walk-ups that look like garbage from a distance, then you get a little closer and they don't look any better.

I knocked once. Then once again. And then I knocked

and I knocked. And then I rang the doorbell. I called her name through the door. I knew exactly what I looked like, but I kept going anyways. I just kept going.

I thought maybe I'd felt something shift in the bag.

When I unzipped it, the chupacabra winced, ducking into the fabric.

It occurred to me that, in this moment, I was probably the closest thing to family it had.

This is for both of us, I said, and then the door finally opened, and I stuffed that motherfucker out of the way. I did my best to smile.

T, he said.

He extended his hand.

I figured at least she'd found herself a handsome one.

It's TeDarus, I said.

Dude was taller than me. Broad-shouldered. With dreads. Probably could've tossed me over the railing.

Bruh, he said, shuffling his feet.

Denise says to tell you she's tired, he said.

Right, I said.

She says she's sorry she had you come around, he said.

Right, I said.

There was sleep on his face. His pajama bottoms were a little saggy.

All of a sudden, I felt ridiculous. I felt like the people you read about in the papers.

You're what she wants, I said, and he made a funny face.

Look, bruh, he said. Wasn't my idea. I told her to come out here.

Whatever, I said. It's fine. She's the one having the baby.

What baby, he said.

I thought about that for a second.

You know how she gets, he said.

Fine, I said.

But it's weird, he said. You know? What you're doing. Coming out. She says you invited yourself.

Denise told me I could come.

Word, he said. And I get it. Pussy's pussy. But, honestly, I don't—

Hey, I said, and loud. Loud enough for her to hear me.

Thanks a lot for answering, I said. Thanks for having Tyrone do your dirty work!

Yo, said the guy. He shifted his feet.

Thanks, I shouted. You don't know how much it means. My dude.

Really, I said. Thank you for fucking all of it.

And I started to say something else, something profound, something game-changing, but that's when his fist hit the bridge of my nose and whatever I had was gone.

Mix was outside in his flip-flops, holding himself under the awning. He had on this ratty bathrobe but his knees poked through the crease. The sky had dimmed into this murky blue, like all of the smog had finally congealed, and our end of the bayou peeked over the mud, slipping straight into the water sloshing beneath it, until the water turned into mud, and the mud congealed into dirt, and that dirt made the bedding for the glossy buildings behind it.

I knew he'd probably been waiting outside for a minute. The blood on my lips had hardened. The swelling'd dimmed to a steady thump. When he saw me with the gym bag, all I could do was smile.

His sandals slapped my way. He snatched the bag from my shoulders.

You shit, said Mix.

I started to tell him that I deserved it—that I'd really, really fucked up.

Then he hit me in the eye.

The pain exploded immediately.

You fuck, said Mix.

I grabbed the hook of his elbow, brought him down with me.

Fucking bitch, said Mix.

He ran his palm across my throat.

I kneed him in the balls.

They came and left, said Mix. They came and they fucking left.

He slipped his wrist under my armpit and I hooked my knee across his chin.

Everyone's always fucking leaving, said Mix. Fucking fuck fuck fuck.

I flipped him. Couldn't help it. He tried to catch himself, but I'm just too big.

I sat on his stomach.

Okay? I said. Okay?

No, said Mix.

God, said Mix. Fuck.

Some cars honked at us. Dogs barked. The air felt crisp on my back. Mix's breathing slowed beneath me, and I loosened my hold on his arms, and the chupacabra poked its head from the bag sprawled open on the concrete.

It looked at the two of us.

It sighed.

Before his brother was locked up, but after he'd gotten kicked out of the house, Mix and I were cooling out in the Whataburger parking lot.

The dude had just beaten the shit out of Mix for like the fourth time in a month. Mix'd called me up that afternoon, but he'd left out the part about the beating. He only asked if I wanted to hang, and I knew from his tone that it needed to happen. So we were sitting in the parking lot, with whoever on the radio, and some sodas in the holders, and our mouths full of burger, when he leaned across his seat, straining against the belt, and put his mouth on mine.

His tongue swam between my cheeks, and I let it. Just for a minute.

He tasted like ketchup. And mayo. And potatoes.

He put his hand in my shorts.

I socked him in the ear.

Jesus shit, I said. I got out and slammed the door behind me.

I took some laps around the parking lot before I came back.

And there Mix was. Sniveling.

He looked like a mess. Like something disgusting. I watched him there crumpling with the paper bag in his lap.

And weirdly, suddenly, and don't ask me how this happens, I saw myself.

So I let him cry for a bit.

I got back in the car.

I put my hand on his shoulder, sort of squeezing around his neck. When that didn't really do anything, I gave him a hug.

Eventually, he sort of fumbled his hands around my shoulders.

We stayed like that for what felt like an hour.

Then he started the car. He pulled us onto the feeder, and back into traffic, and out of the lot.

It could've been midnight but it was probably later. The parking lot had emptied. The only thing moving was the water in the bayou beneath us. Mix sat in his robe, cradling the chupacabra in his hands, and it'd nestled into his stomach, licking the crook of his arm. He'd burrowed his hands into its mane, and it chewed harder than it should've, but Mix didn't seem to care. He kept scratching under its neck.

My phone vibrated in my pocket.

Chingao, said Mix, after a while, and I agreed.

Then the chupacabra's eyes opened completely. It slipped out of Mix's lap, onto the asphalt, and it pranced in a circle. Sizing us up. When it'd made some silent decision, it settled down in front of my feet.

I touched its nose. The chupacabra made a face.

TeDarus, said Mix, and that's when I looked up.

Everyone says this and it's a fucking cliché, but I'd never seen anything like it.

The first few were standing in front of us. Another group stood behind them, waiting in the ranks. They were big and small and fat and tall. Their manes were glossy, with a shimmering sheen.

We were surrounded by chupacabras.

We watched them watching us.

I didn't move. I motioned to Mix. But it was clear that he'd seen them all along.

He started to stand, then changed his mind.

The one we'd found gave us a long look. It twisted its head, between us and them. It arched its back. Popped its legs.

And then it walked toward the rest of them.

And it didn't look back.

One by one, the others followed our chupacabra back toward the bayou.

Mix and I watched them go. We didn't say a word. We watched them plod across the street. We watched them step over the rocks. We watched them walk through the water, past the stream, under the buildings with their smog and their grime, and then the shot-up laundromats, and the broke-down pharmacies, and the gas stations with the low-riders parked out front, and, after all that, they slipped into the forest, and then they were really gone.

LOT

1.

Javi said the only thing worse than a junkie father was a faggot son. This was near the beginning of the end, after one of my brother's marathon binges; a week or two before he took the bus to Georgia for basic training. His friends carried him home from the bars off Commerce, had him slinking around Houston like a stray. Since Ma had taken to locking the door at night, it was on me to let him back in.

At first, she hit him. Asked was he trying to kill her. Was he trying to break her heart.

Later on she took to crying. Pleading.

Then came the clawing. The reaching for his eyes like a pair of stubborn life rafts.

But near the end Ma just stared at him. Wouldn't say a word.

Javi sat on my bed when he told me this. Smelling fresh like he'd just been born.

I asked what he meant, and he looked at me, the first time I think he'd ever really looked at me before.

He told me it didn't matter. It wasn't important.

He told me to go back to sleep.

2.

Ma planned on leaving the restaurant to the three of us, but then Jan had her own thing going on, and she didn't want shit to do with the business, and Javi deployed, and it all came down on me. So I stayed. I slice and I marinate and unsleeve the meat. Pack it in aluminum. Load the pit, light the fire. The pigs we gut have blue eyes. They start blinking when you do it, like they're having flashbacks or something, but after nineteen years of practice one carcass just feels like the next.

Way back when, Ma made Jan responsible for that, for prepping the beef with paprika and pepper, for drowning the carp with the rest of our voodoo, but then my sister met her whiteboy, Tom—working construction in the Heights, way the fuck out of East End—and he stuffed enough of himself inside her to put her in bed with a kid. Which brought our staff to two. Just me and Javi.

Neither of us gave a shit about cooking, but we both cared about eating. Ma had us wrapping beef in pastries, silverware in napkins. Javi taught me how to dice a shrimp without getting nicked. He plucked bills from pockets, cheesing like his life depended on it, and, since he was already nineteen, I followed his lead until Ma finally caught me with the fifties in my sock.

For which Javi took the blame. Ma leered him down a

solid ten minutes before she told him to leave, to pack his shit, to go, to never come back. And he did it.

He went.

Joined the service. Sent postcards from brighter venues.

Now it's just me in the back. Packing aluminum in paper bags. Setting the ovens to just under a crisp. Ma pokes her head in when there's time—the one thing we have too much of—just to ask me if I've got it. If everything's under control.

And the answer's always, always no.

But of course you can't say that.

3.

Come morning I'm in the kitchen around eight. Ma's counting bills, twisting rubber into bundles.

Good night? she asks, and I say, Yeah, same as always, Ma.

She'll nod like she knows what the fuck I'm talking about. Ma learned about suspicion from my father, from lies he'd wooed her away from Aldine with, but then he left for a pack of cigarettes and she gave up snooping entirely.

We don't talk about where I go most nights or how I get back, ever, so I head to the freezer to handle the prep.

Beef's fairly quick. Fish too. Chicken takes the longest. We douse them for a week or so—just drown the carcasses in salt. Ma adds her own seasoning, all pepper and grain and kernel, coating every limb with it. Shit she pulled from her mother, and her mother's mother before her, back when they picked berries in Hanover. Then we stuff it all in some buckets, let them sit for like a day.

It's something our father would do. He'd pitched Ma the restaurant like a pimp, like a hustler.

Think Oaxaca!

Bun and patties, menudo on Saturdays.

The blacks eat chicken so we'll have that, too.

And, sometimes, I like to think that she put up a fight back then, tried to think of another plan.

But a month later they'd already set up shop. Found a shotgun off the freeway, polished it up. Our father served quesadillas and wings and pinto beans, hiring any number of the neighborhood layabouts, his friends, whooping and yelping and eyeing Ma from their stations. Sometimes she'd swat at them, ask who the fuck were they working for. Mostly she let them carry on.

My parents smoked cigarettes on the porch at sunset. Waving at everyone like they had something to smile about.

But Ma couldn't get down with his pails. How they stank up the place. She said we were living in a slaughter-house, that her home smelled like death.

Her kids were another story: Javi and I dipped our toes in the buckets, until Jan saw us, and said to cool it, to cut it out. We kept doing it and she kept catching us.

One time she'd reprimanded us a little too slow. Javi grabbed her, and he dunked her, and he held her until his arm got tired.

Hush, he said, and then again, slower.

4.

Javi sent letters from out east. A photo of some dunes. Some birds. An old fort. White words on gray backgrounds, angled across the card. He'd say how he was doing (fine), bitch about the weather (worse than Houston), ask for more photos of Jan's kid.

Once, he wrote a letter just for Ma. She wouldn't let anyone touch it.

Once, he wrote one just for me.

He asked how Ma was doing, really, and about the baby. And about my plans. Said something about sending me some money. About what he'd do when he got out. He told me to write him sometime, that he'd appreciate it.

So I did that. I wrote him a letter spelling everything out. I wrote about Ma, and the shop, and the school. I wrote about Jan and the baby. I wrote about the Latina girls from Chavez I'd been meeting and fucking, and how that wasn't working out, or how it wasn't what I'd thought it should be, or that there was something else out there maybe, but what that was I couldn't tell him, until I saw him, until he came back home.

I actually wrote that down.

I tossed it in the postbox before I could think about it, before it really messed me up.

But then a letter came for Ma, and then another one after that for Jan. But nothing addressed to me. I never tried again.

5.

I spend most days just trying to keep the place from burning down.

Four stoves, two ovens, three sinks. They're always running. It might actually scare the shit out of anyone who cared to check, but nobody does that with Ma up front, dropping smiles and tossing napkins and asking everyone how their food is.

We get our rush in the afternoon, when the neighborhood shakes itself awake. Same faces every day. Black and brown and tan and wrinkled. The viejos who've lived on Airline forever. The abuelitas who've lived here for two hundred years, and the construction workers from Calhoun looking for cheap eats. The girls from Eastwood my sister left behind. The hoods my brother used to run with downtown.

Occasionally we'll pull in a yuppie. They'd find us on the internet, review us in the weeklies. You can tell from the clothes, the bags. Their shades. How they ask what's on the menu, any specials. Ma would treat them all like God's children.

It's a major event in our week, this pandering. So they get all the stops. And they'll promise to tell their friends, to come back next week, but they sit through their meals with their eyes on the tile and their elbows on their purses so we know they never will.

Ma swears it's the locals that gut us. That we can't keep giving handouts.

I don't know about that though. Change anything too much, it gets harder to keep it alive.

6.

You know the day's almost over when Jan drops in with the kid. I set the burners to low and pop out to kiss him, and she swats at me, tells me to wash my nasty hands. Ma's chatting with the only table occupied, a gaggle of off-duty fags, dressed down.

Ever since she had the baby Jan's been dressing like a nun. Black sleeves. Dresses. The phone company lets her do whatever she wants—because she can enunciate—but if she'd laced those buttons from the beginning she wouldn't be scrounging in the first place.

She talks with Ma while I play with the boy. He's like a sack of potatoes. Fat in the face. There's none of me there, which is fine, but what makes him even luckier's that there's none of his daddy either.

Jan leans across the counter, says things are looking slower. I tell her we've seen worse.

Any worse, she says, and there'll be nothing to see.

It's how she's started talking. Between moving downtown, and living alone, and wilding out and fucking around and ending up with the whiteboy, Jan was the black sheep after she'd gotten hitched, almost as bad as Javi once he'd enlisted. Once the ring hit her finger, she swore the rest of us off. She was always dropping by Next Week, always tied up with the in-laws; until the day she finally brought Tom around the restaurant for lunch, and he laughed at Ma's jokes, and he actually asked me about my life.

But after we ate, and her guy took off for home, Jan

called us both trash. She said we'd embarrassed her. We were the reason she never came around. And Ma didn't even blink—she just said, Go.

But a baby makes everything better.

I ask if Tom's found another job yet, and she tells me he has, a construction gig down in River Oaks. For some billionaire apartment complex by the Starbucks.

So you should have a little extra to kick around, I say. For Ma.

We both look at the kid.

Mom's fine, she says.

Ma's broke.

Business in a place like this, and you're hot about being broke?

You're the one who said it was slow.

Trust me, says Jan. Or her, at least. She's got a plan.

A plan.

Property value's going up, she says. I saw at least two new buildings on the drive over. And some new families in the neighborhood.

By new she means white. We don't even have to say it anymore.

I tell Jan if she thinks we're selling our place, she's who's fucking crazy.

Yours, she says. Or hers?

Ours, I say, and my sister hums that right off, staring out the window.

But anyways, she says. How's the queer thing going?

It's going, I say.

Any prospects?

Stop.

I have to ask.

No one has to say anything.

Jan just shakes her head. She's the only one who talks about it. I don't know if Ma told her, or if Jan just put two and two together, but one day she told me it didn't matter who I was fucking. Out of the blue. She said it wasn't her business, or Ma's business, or anyone's business. She said that Javi never asked for permission. I shouldn't have to answer to anyone.

But she always, always asks. And I give her the same answer every time.

We watch her kid. He's still running in circles, trailing his hand along the counter. When he makes it to the boys by the window, they squeal.

They're all done up. Hair the shade of supernovas. Out of the four of them, three are obviously fucked; the other one's just a little too thick, touched with a shade of aftershave. He'd look like an imposter if he weren't clearly the leader; when Jan's kid stops in front of him, he lifts him by the armpits.

The others squeeze his cheeks. Run their fingers through his hair. They're all in sandals, heels slapping like crocodiles.

The kid's soaking them up, taking it in. And the fags are, too—cooing, like birds, urging him not to grow, grow, grow.

7.

Couple months before he started to turn, Javi got it in his head that he'd teach me to sock a baseball. This was before

Jan's baby, and the military, and the neighborhood's infiltration by money, but after my father left, a time when you could probably look at the four of us and still call us okay. It would've been summer, because he slugged me in my shoulder, said we were going outside, to get my ass off the carpet and take notes on being a man. I was watching a movie, *Princess* fucking *Mononoke,* and he told me I had till he counted to one.

I couldn't hit for shit. Didn't matter that it was dark out. Woofed it even when he stood in front of me, pulling his elbow back just in time.

Useless, he said, after every single shot. You'd spill a water bottle if I put it in your mouth.

But he stayed out there.

He didn't tell me to kick rocks. Didn't deem me obsolete. Didn't manufacture an excuse to disappear. Didn't knuckle me in my ear until blood came out. All that would come later, like he was making up for lost time. But that night, he stayed with me, with the moon whistling and the cars in the road and the grass inching beneath us like caterpillars.

Again, he said, shaking his head, squeezing my shoulder.

8.

The evenings I'm not out chasing ass I'm across the sofa from Ma. We're on the second floor of the property, this joint we used to rent out after Jan left.

Halle Berry's on the television. Boxing the hell out of

some kid. It is cable and it is senseless, but I laugh when Ma laughs, turn sober when she tears up.

By the end of the movie she's finished her tea. She's looking over the commercials, past the credits, through the wall.

Ma, I say, and it spooks her.

She looks at me.

My mother's the only girl in the world who smiles as sad as she does.

Just thinking, she says.

When I ask about what, she says the future.

Your sister and the baby. Your education.

And the restaurant, I say. When she makes her I-don't-know-why-you'd-say-such-a-thing face I say she's my mother, that I'm no dummy.

The moment Javi left, she'd started pushing me toward college. Asking about homework. Meeting with teachers who couldn't have given a shit. And it didn't help that I couldn't care less either; that, in the grand scheme of things, I knew this wasn't helping anyone.

Except eventually I changed my mind.

I thought about Rick and the rest of them.

I can't even tell you why.

And, eventually, my counselor started looking me in the eyes. I still worked the kitchen, but Ma filled in the gaps, covering for me, or hiring the stove by the hour, until I finally got the diploma and she cried at graduation and it became clear that the only place I was going was nowhere.

Money issues aside, leaving the neighborhood meant leaving the shop. Which meant leaving Ma. Leaving her broke and alone. She used to wave this off, tell me Jan was still around, but I grew up with my sister and there's things you don't forget. I even tried community college for a week or three, right on Main Street, sat in the front row and everything, but one day I stopped all that and no one said a fucking thing. No alarms rang. No one called the restaurant. It didn't take long to see that there's the world you live in, and then there are the constellations around it, and you'll never know you're missing them if you don't even know to look up.

Ma's daughter had left her.

Her son had left her.

Her husband had left her.

So I couldn't leave her.

Not that it's worth feeling sorry for.

It's honestly not even sad.

They're only inquiries, Ma says, after a while. The neighborhood's changing.

It's always changed, I say. It'll keep changing.

I'm weighing our options. We might need the money.

My ass, I say. For what?

Watch it, she says.

You know, she says, but that's all she's got.

Ma just starts nodding. Moves her head like she's already made her decision, but she's still willing to hear me out, at least for a little while.

Months after our father left, Ma sat Javi and me in the kitchen, something she never did. Hair all over her face, in last week's nightdress, she looked like Medusa in the pit.

She said if we remembered nothing else she taught us, to know that love was a verb. She had makeup all over her brow. Smears of it on her lips.

When I'd started to open my mouth Javi kicked me under the table. Didn't even change the look on his face.

It is an active thing, she said. Something you have to do.

But now, when she shuts her eyes, I know she's not asleep. I watch until her breathing slows.

Until I know she's finally out.

9.

This next time I'm ready when the realtor shows. Ma's so caught off guard she doesn't have time to lie.

It's actually a lady. Korean, probably, but I'm not the one to know.

Well, she says, smiling at me, but talking to Ma. If this is a bad time—

It's a great time, I say, taking the chair beside Jan. She doesn't even glance at me.

Ma says something about the afternoon rush, but once it's clear that I'm not getting up for anything the suit-lady smiles, dives back into her spiel.

It hurts me to say she was good. Told us who was interested, how much we'd profit. Every now and again, she'd add a quick *but,* as if to show us she was the only person worth trusting here, our only honest apple.

And once she told us everything, she asked if we understood, did we have any questions.

And since none of us wanted to be the one to ask them, she stood, and she smiled, and said it was nice to finally meet me.

She nodded at Ma and then Jan. Told us all to stay in touch.

We told her we would.

10.

When our father split, he took every sound in the house with him. Ma wouldn't talk for another few weeks, at least not to us; so the last things she'd called him were what floated in the air.

Javi and I took note, but we weren't actually worried. He'd left before. They fought, he'd take off, but he'd always materialize by Sunday, frying eggs over salsa on the stove, Beatles wailing on the radio.

But Jan told us that this time was different. That she'd actually talked to him the night he left. She said he called her sometimes, when everyone was asleep. Javi said he knew she was lying because who the fuck would waste their minutes on her, and she looked at him, and she smiled, and she said we'd never see our father again.

When I asked Javi if there was any truth to this, he didn't say anything. He was usually the first one to pop off, calling bullshit even when he knew better—but he just put his hand on my head, and he told me to be tough. That it was the only way a man did things in life.

So I stayed up to see if it was really true. Javi'd already started sneaking out by then, and when Ma caught me by the phone that night she just blinked.

Then it finally did ring.

An alarm went off in my eyes.

I pounced on it, already asking where he'd gone, and when he'd be back, talking and talking, words bursting out of my nose, my ears, but of course it was only my mother's brother, asking who was this, where was Ma, get the fuck off the phone.

11.

I tell Ma that selling the lot is a bad move. We've closed shop for the evening, and the sun bleeds through the windows.

Nothing's been decided, she says, and Jan says Ma doesn't have to do that, she doesn't have to lie.

It's done, Jan says to me now. It's been done for a while.

I tell my sister to shut her mouth, to crawl back into her hole.

Hon, says Ma.

Let him, says Jan. Let him have his say.

Because the sale went final a week ago, says Jan. We'll be out of the building in two weeks at most.

We, I think.

I look at Ma.

She doesn't have to explain it to you, says Jan.

Ma, I say, and she stands up to go, and I know I should follow her but I sit my ass down.

If I tell you what I think, will you listen? says Jan. She's still at the table, knuckles under her chin. Will you be serious for two seconds?

What you think, I say.

Yes. The conclusions I've reached with the data we've acquired.

Tom's got you thinking now? You're the barrio's new psychiatrist?

Let's start with that, she says. You think you're special. You think you're special since you live where you live, but no one else in this dump really gives a shit about you.

Bravo.

You think if you don't say anything about it, this place will just stay how it's been. You think that's a good thing. You think it means you won't have to change.

You think, says Jan, that *he's* coming back. Like, if we all stay in place, he'll stick his head up from six feet under. We'll just rewind everything. Click him back into rotation.

But here's the thing, she says. Javi's not coming back. Javi's not here because he's gone. Gone. And as soon as you pop your little-brother bubble, and you actually *look* at—

And this is why we should sell, I say. That's your reason?

What reason, she says.

Because you didn't fucking like him. You never fucking liked him.

Jan frowns at this. She folds her arms. It puts another thirty years on her.

No, she says. We should sell because your mother needs the money. Because neither of us has it, and the neighborhood's buying out.

Just her, I say. *My* mother? You think she won't give half to you?

She reaches across the counter to put her hand on my cheek. Massages it, one finger between the other.

I wouldn't take it, she says.

I wouldn't want it, she says. Because you two need it. You need it.

But if you can think of a better way to fix this, she says, you need to tell me. Right now. You need to speak up.

Jan fondles my face. I can feel it burning. It's been years since my sister touched me, let alone with warmth.

Her fingers are sharp. A little callous.

Get out, I say.

Ah, says Jan. You're mad.

We're closing shop, and I've got dishes to wash. And you smell like vomit. Get out.

My sister looks me over like she's deciding something.

Fine, she says.

But you need to start making plans, she says. You need to figure out where you're staying next. She's getting older, and I've got a full house, so you're damn sure not living with me.

The nickel I throw skips over the counter, across a tabletop, right by some silverware, and into her palm.

Don't ask me how. I'd meant to hit her in the eye.

But she catches it, and she smiles, again, and she slips it in her purse on her way out the door.

12.

Javi was dead for a month and four days before his first sergeant made it out to the restaurant.

I don't even remember what I was doing, but Ma met the guy at the register like any other customer. She had no idea.

This is what kills me, more than anything else.

Dumb luck, is what his sergeant called it. A car crash on post. Only he said it like it really was dumb. Completely illogical. The stupidest thing he'd ever heard.

When Ma asked him to sit, he told her no, he really had to go. He'd just wanted to come by. To tell her personally.

Ma asked if he wanted anything to take with him. He said no, he really did need to leave. She told him anything on the menu, anything up there, it didn't matter what, just tell her and she'd fix it for him.

I don't know what he said to that. I haven't gone and asked. But what I do know is that he ended up leaving with nothing.

Jan came over that night. She left the baby with Tom.

We closed shop for the rest of the week, had the funeral that weekend. Tom and his folks showed. Some of Ma's friends were there, overdressed like toucans in too-tight dresses, crying in heels and mascara and polish. A handful of Javi's boys made it out, a couple of guys in uniform. One of them asked me if I was his brother. He shook my hand.

Ma just stared at the casket. I thought maybe she'd kick it or push it or pull out her eyes, but she did not.

Two weeks later, doors were back open. Jan told Ma to stay off her feet, but our mother said that wasn't necessary.

And anyways, it wasn't possible. We honestly couldn't afford it.

13.

The day we sign the lot away, Jan comes straight from work. Ma's in a seat by the window, lost in this dress I've never seen before and haven't since. She asks if I want to stay awhile—to look over the numbers myself—but I say no thanks, I'm fine, let me know when you're finished.

14.

I used to think my brother would come back at night, like he used to, only this time he'd be dressed like some hijo de papi, like someone with a mother and a sister and a brother he loved. He'd have a wife by then. Somebody with a laugh. And he'd blush when he introduced us, pointing out the house's trinkets, the floors he used to sweep. They wouldn't have a kid yet, but it'd be on the way, and when

Ma asked him who'd watch the baby he'd look at me, nod, squeeze my shoulder. Say, Who else.

He'd really know me by then. He'd know who I was.

But Javi did come back on leave, once, a few months before that final deployment.

Ma closed the restaurant for the weekend. Rushed around the place making sure everything looked right—that his room was in order, that the cabinets were clean, redusting and revacuuming and all the shit we usually ignore. Jan told her to settle down, that it was Javi, not Jesus, but Ma told her to shut up. One of the only times she's let my sister have it since the baby.

You take care of what's yours, was all Ma said. They may leave but when they come back you take care of them.

He took a cab from the airport. Let himself in. Hugged Ma and she instantly started to cry. We did the handshake thing. He kissed Jan and he shook her husband's hand and he snatched her baby up from the carpet so fast that everyone flinched a little bit.

Javi looked thicker. Darker. Not gruff or monosyllabic or any of that shit, but there was something there that wasn't there the last time we'd seen him. Or maybe something that wasn't there at all.

We made his favorite dinner, jerk shrimp with potatoes, and he tried to jump in the kitchen but Ma told him to stop playing.

For finally being home, it felt like the end of something.

After dinner, he stood up. Yawned. We'd have him the whole weekend, he said, but the flight had been long. He was tired. Ma told him to get to bed, quickly, we'd see him in the morning, and before too long I followed him upstairs, left Ma and Jan in the dark of the kitchen.

My room was his room. I knocked before I went in. Javi'd collapsed across the mattress, away from the door, and he smiled when I touched him, when I took the floor beside him.

Well, I said. I didn't finish my sentence and he didn't follow up. We sat next to each other, just being brothers.

After a while, he said I'd grown up. Gained some weight in my face.

I'm fat, I said, and he said no, just a little weight, which was what I'd needed, and the hand he put on my shoulder felt like brambles.

We sat there for a while.

I wrote you a letter, I said, like in those fucking movies.

I know, said Javi.

And then he shut up.

Okay, I said.

So how was it over there, I said.

He didn't answer. And it was so long before he said something that I figured he'd forgotten me.

It was just another thing to do, he said, in a different place. It's like I could've just stayed in East End.

But you see how other people live, he said. And you really can't help them if they don't want it.

That's one thing I've learned, he said. That's what I've gotten out of this.

And it looks like nonsense now, like Santa Claus when you're older, but that's when I told him I'd been sleeping with boys.

I told him about the one from the library. About the one from the coffee shop. I told him these things, how I'd tried it with Cristina and Maribel, with LaShon and her sister; and how it hadn't worked, with any of them, even when they'd stared me down, arms crossed. I watched Javi's face for something to click or contort or scrunch itself into oblivion but it did not. It didn't happen.

He said nothing, and I was finished talking.

And I didn't feel it when he slapped me.

I saw his palm coming, but didn't know it until my shoulder hit the ground, until I looked up to see him staring.

And the thing that I remember about my brother, clearer than what he wore on the day he left, or the cracks he made about our uncle when he came to visit Ma, or the way that he laughed or the color of his eyes or his scent or his funeral, is the look on his face while I lay on the carpet.

When he didn't get up, and I didn't get up, I rolled myself over, made a pillow on the floor, and my brother, here and gone, fell asleep on my bed.

SOUTH CONGRESS

The pretty ones always came looking for pills. Blonde and dazzling. Fresh from the Roxy. Glittered dresses and caramel lip gloss, and Raúl couldn't help but drool, just a little, as they slumped through the Corolla's open passenger window, poking the length of his seat belt. In the passenger seat, Avery was suave, or whatever passed for that at forty—all Yes ma'am, and Wouldn't you know, beautiful, and Of course I saved my good shit for you—but it was Raúl who blushed when they howled his name, days past drunk, *Hoe*-la Rah-*hool,* Did you *miss* us Rah-*hool,* Give me a kiss over *here* Rah-*hool,* until Avery finally waved them away, twenties folded under his palms, yelling at the kid to drive and keep his eyes on the fucking street.

Raúl could usually tell which drugs they were looking for just by the corner they chose. He'd gotten good at that. They'd park on Congress for however long it took, until the pickups cruised under the streetlamps on McKinney—or the bimmers by Rusk, the purple minivans near the community garden—and he'd lean into the backseat for the little black JanSport, sifting through baggies sealed with rubber bands and tape. Everything had a label. It was Avery's call who got what bag. Because everyone, according to Avery, had a type, some nasty little vice.

Kush was all the bums could afford. Spice for the Arabs bussing tables on Gray. The doctors asked for coke and the valets asked for coke and the oil and gas crowd wanted whatever cost the most. E for the housewives, hash for the doormen, and pot for anyone who didn't know what they were looking for until Avery asked respectfully, demurely, if a little cannabis would do. The girls from the Roxy asked for their usual, a pack of poppers, and Raúl unearthed the baggies from his jacket like a budget magician.

Raúl didn't deal, in the beginning, or ever. He just drove. At first the roads made no sense but eventually he figured them out. Fannin hooked into Dallas. La Branch sat across from Austin. Streets ran in conjunction, a tangle of dirty shoelaces. It wasn't long before Avery stopped quarterbacking from the passenger seat, and Raúl didn't mind the silence, he actually sort of welcomed it, until he looked over to find him snoring, dead to the world.

Some nights they just cruised and cruised. Stopping and turning. Breaking before the expressway.

But mostly they had business. A drop here, a sure thing there. They'd wait until the cops packed it in, creeping around the same avenues. Then one evening, early on, Raúl blew through a light, and a siren wailed a lone note before the flash went off behind him. He nearly shit himself. Months and months of riding dirty all over Houston, and here he was: about to be deported for missing a red.

Except Avery woke up. He rolled down his window, called the cop by name—*Jeremiah! They done switched you up!*—and Officer Jeremiah Stewart blinked, stuttering, before he tightened his belt and cracked his knuckles and hunched over the passenger door like he'd been looking for something himself.

They jawed about football and cousins and brisket. Avery asked about the wife, their garden in the Ward. The cop said something about Avery's son, and Avery blew right by that with a wave, said the kid was a man now, better off than the both of them. They talked and they talked, and Raúl pinched himself, a little drowsy, until the cop nodded his way, asking Avery who that was. And Avery smiled with all of his teeth before he said, My nephew, obviously.

He was still cheesing hours later. A rolling guffaw like an avalanche.

Everybody out here looking, he said. And don't know when to open their eyes.

Uh-hunh, Raúl nodded. Uh-hunh, uh-hunh, uh-hunh.

Avery would pick him up after dark. They'd creep along roads Raúl'd stepped through earlier, static if not for the streetlights, the monorail. So late that no one was out walking unless they had to, and the silhouettes between alleys looked like something off the television.

Their supplier was a stocky Greek. Damian Dukakis. Damo to associates. Raúl didn't know about Greece, couldn't have found it on a globe with his finger on the

Aegean, but standing in Damo's condo, you'd have thought they'd landed in Athens. Portraits weighed the walls. Butter clogged his nose, wafting in from the kitchen. Occasionally, a little girl flashed through the kitchen, corralled when an older woman sped around the corner, and Damo'd stop midsentence, snapping his pudgy fingers in Raúl's face.

They'd leave with a week's supply. Come back the next to distribute Damo's cut. His yard sat under a bed of trees, an oasis right in the center of town, and Avery'd shake his head on their way out the door, saying Damo's good people, to Raúl, who hadn't asked.

Family man, said Avery. Got a daughter, an old lady. Been pushing for twenty-two years now and not one fuckup.

Or just one, he said. Small thing. Couple kids came sniffing around. Damo plugged their noses.

Man knows what time it is, said Avery. Most boys out here don't.

All Raúl knew was that most boys looked nothing like them. Most boys slung dope in gas-station parking lots. Most boys slipped half their cut to whatever schmuck took them on. Headphones on their domes, always young and black and mean and smoking. He didn't know what they saw when they scoped him and Avery, a dirty old man and a Guatemalan in a Corolla, but he knew what they couldn't have guessed—that they were taking in more than a couple grand a night. And from all parties, too: white, brown, red, and yellow.

Desire don't *discriminate,* said Avery. Desire's gonna swallow every motherfucker out here.

So we don't discriminate neither, said Avery. We're equal opportunity pharmacists!

Raúl worked other jobs before this one, but his English was rough and the city wasn't waiting on him. He'd ground meat for a Thai diner, strung hangers at a dry cleaner. Twenty-hour days, six days a week. Whatever cash they paid him, if they paid him at all, was just enough for bus fare and maybe a grubby taco. He'd considered whoring himself at one of the clubs set up off Elgin, but the other guys dissuaded him, bitching about the pay, and when Raúl glanced at the clientele, balding white dudes in graying suits, he decided he wasn't quite desperate enough to let one of them inside of him.

This was after nearly a year of sitting around his aunt's apartment, a dilapidated piss-yellow complex downtown. Pacing up Alabama, conjugating English verbs under his breath. The buildings always impressed him, so tall in the business district that he'd squint and shut his eyes as if maybe then he'd catch their peaks. The Nigerian vendors behind the complex had come to recognize him, and sometimes he'd slip into their stalls, hearing out their pitches for earrings and DVDs. Raúl never bought shit, but he always listened. Their accents were like potholes. The clicking of consonants dulled to a thud. He'd offer a thumbs-up, and they'd offer theirs back.

His mother'd sent him up from Villa Nueva, and his father was who knew where.

He lived with his aunt as a favor to her sister. The aunt

worked in a hospital, bucketing piss and blood for years, but eventually the ladder presented itself and now she was some doctor's secretary. She was grateful to her sister, who'd stayed behind for their parents, so that she could flee, but the years had passed and her brow had furrowed, and eventually she realized she didn't have to hold on to that. She could admit that she hadn't much liked her. And she didn't much like Raúl either. He was too dark, always gurgling his words. He spoke too quietly. He never washed the dishes. And no matter how many times or what tone she used, he always left the seat up, like she was back on the old shift, like she wasn't doing him and his whore mother a solid.

Eventually Raúl found himself on a day crew, after a Mexican with a wrench spotted him drifting up the block. They held eye contact for a few waxy seconds, and the man asked in impeccable English if he was employed. He told Raúl to come back tomorrow, crack of dawn, and Raúl told his aunt about the encounter that evening, his first strike of luck in weeks and weeks. She told him he must not have opened his mouth.

He showed the next morning. Dirty jeans, white shirt. The man did not. Raúl stood among the smoking workers for a while, looking for a conversation to fold himself into, and when it became clear that they either couldn't or wouldn't hear him, he asked, not impolitely, about the man he'd spoken to yesterday.

Accident, said another guy, not even looking up from his coffee. Faggot fell off a chimney.

So Raúl was the replacement. Lucky he'd shown up.

What they did was roof houses. Not in the neighborhoods that clearly needed roofing—the ones with more black people than he'd ever seen in his life—but the other ones. The quiet ones. The ones with trees bursting from lawn-lined sidewalks and children walking in groups, chaperoned by wide women in orange vests and hard hats. At lunch they'd sit and watch the convoy pass. Sometimes a kid waved, and the men would wave back, until the chaperone grabbed the child's wrists, shooting the workers a look.

Raúl wasn't great with a hammer, but he figured that if he eliminated a nail a day he'd at least look like an asset. Maybe. A handful of old hires swung by to check on him, and they'd see the nail, and they'd see Raúl. And they didn't laugh or frown. They shrugged. Squeezed his shoulder.

He spent the rest of that day and a couple more hammering.

It was something to do.

But then one morning the next week, the job was over. He loafed around their meeting spot for a while, nodding at everyone else left off the worksheet memo for a new project. When it was clear that the ship had moved on, and that he wouldn't be paid, he walked back home beside the steady belch of traffic.

They met on a lazy afternoon. Raúl had stepped outside the apartment for a cigarette, although really it wasn't the smoke he needed so much as a break from so many different tongues and that crushed feeling he got whenever he shut his eyes. The AC in the apartment had taken the day off. The roaches under the carpet had overtaken the countertop. He was watching a Jehovah's Witness work her way up the block when the little black Corolla slid into the lot behind her.

That lot belonged to a series of new lofts. Glossy and refurbished. Lawn chairs on the balconies. Raúl didn't even look at those buildings, because they made his stomach pop. They made him think of murder. A whiteboy in joggers skipped out of the garage, glancing both ways before he leaned into the Corolla.

Raúl watched them talk. He watched the exchange of hands. And then the car peeled off, and the whiteboy skipped away, like he hadn't just handed something like two grand to a stranger. The whole transaction took less than two minutes. The little Jehovah lady in the shawl hadn't even crossed the road yet.

A few days later, but not too soon, Raúl found himself in the same spot, broad day, smoking. He didn't have a plan.

Then the Corolla pulled into the lot. The driver's window drooped, revealing a black man in shades. Grizzled, with a mustache as dark as any Raúl'd ever seen.

Can I he-*elp* you, he said, and Raúl just swallowed. He said he didn't know.

The man looked at Raúl's tattered flip-flops, his unwashed hair. He asked if he was looking for pot.

No, said Raúl.

The man asked if he was looking for blow, and Raúl told him he wasn't. The man asked if he was looking for dust, and Raúl told him he wasn't. The man asked if he was looking for X, and Raúl told him he wasn't. The man asked and asked and asked and asked and Raúl shook his head, a little dizzier for the effort.

So, said the man. You just popped over to my spot to chat.

Raúl peeked into the car. He said he was looking for work.

The man asked if Raúl worked for Jacob, did he work for Screwtop, or Lacy, or Tom-Tom.

Raúl knew what he wanted to say, but he didn't know how to say it in English.

No, he said.

Then what the fuck, said the man.

Raúl swallowed again. He said he was looking for work.

Downtown traffic had begun to wake up. Raúl could spot his aunt's window from the concrete below. The Nigerians behind them yelled obscenities at passersby, waving purses and blankets and key chains from Beijing. A school of schlubby bankers in ties crossed the road, cell phones at their ears, gophers in motion.

The man just stared at Raúl through the car window.

Then he sighed. Shook his head. He slipped off his shades, unearthing a pair of tired eyes.

Avery extended his hand. He asked if Raúl had a name, or had he left that at home with his sense.

. . .

Avery knew all their buyers' names, and eventually Raúl did, too.

They sold to the postman who never wore socks. They sold to the sturdy little woman in a flowing hijab. They sold to the cabbies, to the line cooks, and to a Pakistani gentleman in a long robe.

Occasionally they broke a little off for the homeless. Damo shook his head whenever they tried to justify it, but they overcharged the club kids, so he never gave them grief. They'd sit in his living room counting out the profit, and Damo only said he really hoped they were proud of themselves.

Avery told him he had no idea.

It baffled Raúl that the people who bought from him left their homes, left their couches and their kids and their fridges and their televisions. To come out here. These stinking, fucking streets. The filthy heft of Texas Avenue and the sewage clogged on Fannin and the twilight at the end of every godforsaken intersection.

But Raúl didn't ask questions. He didn't say shit about it.

It's hubris, said Avery, one day, apropos of nothing. They'd been waiting on a drop for an hour and a half, after the girl swore she'd left the rest of the cash back at her place. She'd been dressed in Peanuts pajamas, clicking through her phone. Avery smiled, told her to take as long as she needed, and the moment she peeled off in her jeep he let out a groan.

Raúl didn't know hubris. He hadn't heard of that word. He'd been practicing his English with Avery whenever business was slow, stuttering through chitchat until it tasted less like rocks. He asked Avery what it meant.

Don't worry about it, said Avery. We'll never have the pleasure.

When business was slow, Avery had stories.

Avery had stories like no one had stories. Stories about coming up in the Ward. Stories about Frankfurt and Rome from when he was in the Army. Stories about how they booted him for fucking some guy's wife. Stories about heroin and the story about his first sale and some stories about his kid, college boy now, Christ bless his mother. Raúl never learned Avery's son's name, he wasn't privy to that information, but he learned a lot of other things about him.

Avery's son was an Eagle Scout. Avery's son was so tall that he could fit in his father's clothes. The year he turned twelve, Avery's son came up with a plan to end homelessness, and he shared it with Avery and his mother in the kitchen. The year he turned eighteen, Avery's son crashed his ride, but only because he was worried about the drivers in the next lane. Avery's son lived less than a couple blocks away, and Avery never saw him, he had no idea what he was up to.

Should be at Texas Southern still, said Avery. 'Bout your age, but cleaner. Less smelly.

Mother's still in the Ward, said Avery. Just didn't work with us. You know how that is. Her new thing's a mechanic.

I told her she had her a street man, said Avery. Told her she's moving down the chain now, and she just clicks her tongue at me like, Duh.

White women, said Avery, they love that shit. A street man. The Arabs, too. Prettiest dish I ever saw was Lebanese, and it really makes sense, the Bible was full of them. Saw her walking through the mall, stepping out the bathroom. Had the sheet on her head and everything, but it didn't matter, she glowed right through it.

Glowed, said Avery. Almost didn't sell to her, because I'm like, *fuck*. If *you* can't kick it, what about the rest of us?

No hope, said Avery. No hope.

Kid doesn't call, said Avery. But I know he looks after himself.

I know how it is, said Avery. People got to make their own choices.

But, he said.

I ever saw him out here? Buying from us?

Don't know what I'd do, said Avery.

Actually, said Avery, I'd break his neck. I'd break his motherfucking neck with my own two hands.

They were waiting for another drop on McKinney, to a house party of swingers huddled up in an attic, when Avery asked Raúl for the first time, was this what he saw himself doing his whole life?

Young thing like you, said Avery, I'd choke a toddler

for the time. Doesn't matter if you're a spic. You're basically taking over the country.

Raúl sunk into the headrest. In the few months they'd been working together, his future had come up once or twice. What he planned on doing. Was he looking for anything else. The money'd been more than enough for him to stay, to say nothing of his aunt, who'd stopped asking where it came from. And the one thing he could never call the man was unfair: Avery had taken him in and showed him the score. He gave him a fair cut and sometimes more than that.

It'd be one thing if you weren't smart, said Avery. If you were a fucking idiot, I'd say live fast, live fast. But you're not a fucking idiot. You're not smart, but you're not that.

These evenings were one thing Raúl knew he'd remember: reclining with an old black man, inching along the avenue, listening to him talk.

And what if you find yourself a little señorita, said Avery. Or a Pablito. Whatever. I don't care. Can't take six steps in this city without kicking a brown baby. And then what'll they do when you get locked up? Twelve years for a backpack of dealer's special? You hear what I'm saying? You fucking listening?

Then, one day later, they were making their rounds.

Raúl knew the roads like he'd paved them by then. Their buyers knew his name, and sometimes he asked how they were doing. Avery would bitch at him about getting too familiar—be kind, sure, but keep it in your pants—but Raúl knew it wouldn't hurt, and anyways, he needed the practice.

He'd started smiling at their regulars. They'd started saying they'd see him later.

But he and Avery were just driving, making their stops between Shepherd and the bars, when they saw the young man on the corner, loitering but looking.

They usually let the junkies go. They were a bad deal. They were the ones who'd pull a gun on you, the addict weeks out of a kick. But Raúl had already pulled onto Waugh when Avery told him to stop, to turn right the fuck around.

Raúl looked at the straggler. Then he looked at Avery.

The young man was haggard. Scrawny in a tattered Hawaiian button-down.

Raúl pulled into reverse, and the two of them sat, watching, until the man saw them park, and he shuffled over, hands chunked in his pockets. He was clearly, clearly strung out. Clearly, clearly in a bad way.

Avery didn't say much about it. He just opened the car door. He opened the door, got out, and walked right up to him. Raúl watched the two of them talk, and he tried reading their lips, and then he realized he didn't have to do that. All he needed was their faces.

Avery's was expressionless and the young man's was too. But different. Sadder. And then Raúl had an understanding that socked him in the rib of his nose.

Avery slapped the young man.

Raúl watched from the window as Avery fell on top of him. Whaling on his face. He hit the young man and he hit the young man and he hit the young man and he hit him. He closed his fists, and hit him again. He put his shoulders into it, really grinding down. He didn't cuss or grunt or grimace, and if Raúl had thought about getting out of the car, to break the thing up, dragging Avery away from the kid—who wasn't even crying, who didn't look like he had any feelings about it at all—then it was a brief, fleeting idea that whooshed right out of his head.

Because Raúl knew he was watching something sacred. A story as old as the earth.

When it was finally over, Avery stood.

He looked at the young man who spit blood on the ground. Then he limped back to the car. The kid looked like a broken fortune cookie.

Before Raúl could even open his mouth, Avery asked what the fuck he was looking at.

He told Raúl to drive already.

He told Raúl they had places to be.

The next evening, Raúl showed up at the meeting place, South Congress and Washington, just north of Discovery, a little south of Montrose, and, lo and behold, no Corolla, no Avery.

He was not entirely surprised.

He stood around in the dark, just soaking into the background. The vendors had started packing their wares, and he watched them slip trinkets and pirated discs into bags. He couldn't see the sky for the buildings, but he looked toward it anyways.

After another hour passed, Raúl rubbed his shoulders, chilly all of a sudden, and started the long walk to Damo's condo off of Elgin.

He reached the gravel pathway with the plants up in front. He didn't know their names, but he'd seen them all before: their purples and their yellows and their light greens and their blues. Standing on the doorstep, he peered through the window, at a man eating dinner with a woman and a child. Raúl knocked four times, and Damo answered on the fifth.

His mouth was full of something. He nodded Raúl off of the porch, shutting the door behind him.

Avery's done, said Damo, chewing.

His lips were greasy. Raúl glanced through the drapes, at the sliver of the lady at the table, the little girl reaching for bread. He opened his mouth, and he closed it, and Damo didn't try to fill it with words.

Done, said Raúl. Or done-done?

Damo stared at Raúl for a very long second.

Done-done, he said. He nodded toward the road. The bushes on the porch had started to shudder, shaking their fronds all over the pavement.

I might have a little work though, said Damo. If you want it.

Raúl looked back into the window.

Small-time, said Damo. Nothing big. Same circuit though. Won't have to learn any new names.

The little girl had gotten her piece of bread. She bit off a glob, letting the rest fall to the floor. Her mother said something about it, something Raúl couldn't understand, but it made the girl laugh and then her mother was laughing beside her, wrapping her arms around the kid, shielding her from the porch. Damo turned around to watch his family through the window, and Raúl hugged himself, too, because it really had gotten cold.

NAVIGATION

1.

It started how you'd think, with this whiteboy throwing up in an alley. I'd pulled a job at a taqueria dumping pig guts out back. The cooks gave me grunt work, the way they do when you're starting out, like when my father had Javi and me pinching the shells off shrimp back in the restaurant as kids. It didn't matter that I'd been fixing mole in Ma's kitchen for years; I was short on money.

My managers looked like gauchos. Porno mustaches, bloated frames. They read my name and they saw my face and they pointed to the dishes. One of them told me I looked like a pinche negrito, y probablemente ni siquiera hablaba español, and I wanted to snatch his ears off but then I'd be out of a check.

So I should've left the whiteboy outside alone. I had enough on my plate.

But I stayed. Watched him heave. When he finished I came back with a glass of water.

He took me home. Dude had these little hairs climbing

his belly. His eyes got wide at how furry my legs are. When we finished he gulped at the air in the room, he asked for my name as we were sliding down the futon, and when he couldn't pronounce it the whiteboy gave me a new one.

He lived in a condo on Navigation. Said he stayed there because *this* was the *real* Houston. This Houston came with needles in the grass, but he said I was lucky, lucky to have it all in front of me. I told him if somebody gave me an out, they wouldn't have time to finish their sentence.

His bedroom was nice and the building was nicer. Wood flooring. Green walls. Like the inside of an avocado. I remembered when the lot had been cleared for the building's construction, when it was just a busted Mattress Center I went to once with Ma, but then the whiteboy started asking me what was wrong, and I said it was nothing, I was gassed, he should be proud of himself.

I grabbed my kicks and left is what should've happened next. That was my thing. And I did dip out, eventually.

But the whiteboy told me he had a job; he needed help with his Spanish because he was gunning for some promotion. He temped at some nonprofit over on Pease, a house for battered refugees. One of those places where everyone's lived through everything. They needed help getting papers, with reaching their people back home, but if he couldn't understand them then he couldn't do much about it. What he really wanted was this position upstate, way out in Dallas, but they'd stuck him in the Second Ward.

The whiteboy told me I could expedite the process. Give him some lessons. Help him help the rest of the world.

I gave him this look like maybe I'd just beat his ass instead. Case his place for fun. It would be so easy.

He asked how much I made dumping napkins. He said he could double it. We'd keep it up as long as we had to. I asked why he didn't just find someone else, someone official, and he said I was already in his bed.

It's one of those moments where I could've done the good thing. Apropos of nothing. Hooked him up, just for the sake of doing it.

I told him for fifty a session I'd think on it.

2.

Meanwhile the taqueria was eating me alive. It was an ultra-retro dive, the kind with barbacoa roasting at dawn. A line of construction types looped the building every morning just to walk like twelve plates home to their kids. We had a guy whose job was sweeping people off of the sidewalk, waving them onto Leeland when the crowd shot through the doors. But somehow the gabachos knew about us too, and by midafternoon we looked a lot less like el D.F. and more like the U.N.

One day nobody was manning the counter, and some blondie yelled to the back for chilaquiles, and when no one else looked up I told the guy we didn't do that. He was a snake in a suit. Glasses tucked in his pocket and everything. He gave this slow nod, like, Well, okay, we'll see.

I was sweeping under the fryers when one of the managers asked for a minute. Something'd come up. Could we touch on it outside. I thought that he'd ask me some bunk about my hours, but when we made it to the back he grabbed me by the throat.

Next time a customer asks for something, he said, you find it. Claro?

I felt like a bobblehead.

I needed the money.

I picked up the phone at Ma's that night, told the whiteboy I was free after ten.

3.

Long story short, this guy was hopeless. Doomed. It took four, five days to stuff the *o* into his *hola.*

We started with greetings. He had so many questions. He wanted to know why he couldn't use *usted* with everyone. He wanted to know why the *x* had to be silent. He wanted to know why every morning had to be bueno.

Some days are just bad, he said. Some people live their whole lives and not a single good thing happens to them.

I told him those were just the rules. He should follow them unless he had something new to say.

I thought he'd bow out, because it really wasn't worth it, but what he did was take notes. He wrote it all down.

Vámonos, I said.

Bamanos, said the whiteboy.

Vámonos. *V.* Think *volcano.*

Bamanos.

No. *Vulcan. Velociraptor.*

Right. Bamanos.

That's how we did it. Had us a full-stop barrier.

And the people at his shelter—on the trains from Tapachula? San Pedro Sula?

Forget about it. They wouldn't be talking to him anytime soon.

I told him this. I told him not to get his hopes up. He rubbed my earlobe with his fingers, said that was where I came in.

Hey, I said, don't get too comfortable.

Cómodo, said the whiteboy. Cómodo?

Correcto.

So we kept it up.

And the whiteboy always paid me afterwards.

And we'd always, always, always, always end up in bed.

Lo siento.

Las siento.

Negative. Lo. Lo.

Las siento.

Weeks passed, then months. We moved from greetings to goodbyes. We brushed by commands. We jumped back to directions. I told him about my father living who the fuck knew where. About my brother in the ground. About Ma and I, stuck in East End, scrambling to keep everything together in a home we no longer owned. The whiteboy told me about his sisters, about his parents in Alamo Heights, and when I asked how many guys he'd been with before me he told me about an ex, some genius over at Rice.

He asked if I was out. I told him I didn't know what that meant. He asked if I'd thought about abandoning Houston, and I said if I had I'd have done it by now.

I kept my head down at the job. Did what I was asked to do. The kitchen was sloppy, utterly inefficient, but every now and again one of the cooks asked for a hand—with temping the oil, with keeping the cow heads intact, or some other no-brainer thing they should've known how to do.

They'd laugh afterwards, pat me with their gloves. Smear all that grease on the back of my tee.

Mostly I wiped benches. My bosses spat on the tile I mopped, asked how my day was going.

I kept my mouth shut about it, kept my eyes on the ground. Because if someone else put their hands on me, I didn't know what I'd do.

Creo que sí.

Creole.

Creo, creo.

Creole, creole.

I started spending my nights with the whiteboy. Dropped whatever scraps I stole from the job over at Ma's. Then took the sidewalk lining Milby on the way to his condo, just before the neighborhood dips into the bayou, and most nights the whiteboy met me at the door; he'd reheat a bowl of whatever he'd ordered for dinner.

We continued our education.

At some point I stopped jumping when he touched me.

At some point the whiteboy started rolling his *r*'s.

At some point I decided I'd make him fluent, however long that took. We would see that through.

4.

Then one night, after a long day, we were rehashing phrases. Things he'd been hearing on his day-to-day. He'd started having piecemeal conversations at work, putting names and addresses together.

The whiteboy told me about the woman who came to Texas in the trunk of a Chrysler, who worked off her debt by dancing in the Galleria.

He told me about the man who'd sold his oldest daughter to traffickers to get his youngest into Brownsville, and how, months later, he still hadn't found either of them.

He told me about the little girl who hadn't said anything, just touched his cheek, rubbing the skin between her fingers, and how after she'd done that he knew no matter how much money he brought in or where he put her family up or how much relief they signed off for, he couldn't do anything to help her at all.

One night, we had a six-pack between us, and his legs on my stomach, which should've been awkward for us. We weren't even fooling with English by then. I was filling in his blanks.

Te amo, I said.

Te amo.

Nice. Good. Te amo.

Te amo.

Right.

Sí.

I laughed in his face, told him to say it again.

I dumped garbage all day, taught my whiteboy at night.

This is how things happen. Even for us.

5.

A few weeks later, he got the promotion.

His supervisor said it wasn't like he was a natural. But out of all the whiteboys they had on hand, he was the closest to whatever they needed.

A position had opened up out in Dallas, if he wanted it. He had a few days to decide.

Of course we had to celebrate. We sat at his table, sober for once, and I told him that was great. He'd probably enjoy himself.

He made this face like that was the wrong response.

I knew what he'd ask, and I answered before he said it.

The whiteboy said I knew I could come too, come with him, and I told him I did.

The whiteboy said this was it, what we'd been working toward, and I told him it may have been.

The whiteboy said there was nothing left for me in Houston, he said that I didn't have to punish myself, and he said my name, my actual name, and I didn't have the words for that.

I stretched my cheeks as far as they'd go. Put a hand on his thigh.

I grabbed my socks and my cap and my belt and I left and he did not put up a fight.

This is how easy it is to walk out of a life. I'd always wondered, and now I knew.

I didn't see him before he took off.

Who knows what he's doing now.

6.

But a week or two later, I was working the night shift, scrubbing blood off the floor, when one of my managers asked for a word.

I'd already decided to put him in the dirt if he touched me. Someone, somewhere in Houston needed a fry cook. I'd twirl signs on the street. Dance on the curb in a phone suit.

He put his hand on my shoulder, and I clinched for the punch.

He told me they'd fired a couple of fatheads for pocketing tips. He called them idiot cabrones, as if he weren't one himself.

But we need a guy who has experience, he said.

We'd start you slow, he said. Behind the stove. Work you up from the bottom.

You're asking me to cook for you, I said, and he shrugged, said, If that's what you want to call it.

I'm asking you to do yourself a solid, he said.

And if this were a different story, a story about something else, a story where we did the things we know we need to do, I'd have smiled real wide, the same as with the whiteboy, and with a little more feeling, or maybe a different one entirely. But I just put my hand on his shoulder, and I squeezed around the edges, and I loudly, gracefully, told him to go fuck his mother.

PEGGY PARK

Micah turned pro and the rest of us went regular. Games started at ten past four. Sometimes we'd fuck around and wait an extra fifteen, if the rain on Scott was heavy enough to slow the rails downtown, and that's where our guys pulled up from, or at least the niggas you wanted on base, since of course the neighborhood's got idle feet all over but mostly we were too fucked-up or too strung out or too in our feelings, or too busy scrapping in the parking lots on Wheeler, or groping each other in the garages downtown, and if you weren't already there then you were on your way but for an hour or three on Wednesday nights we were present, clear in the moment.

Jacoby manned the upper outfield. Now he's a mechanic or some shit. The bat was too heavy for Lenny and today he's a drunk holding court on Westheimer. Kendall threw, caught, and tagged, then he had a son at seventeen, and then he slit his wrists over custody when he divorced like fourteen years later. On the other side of the pitch, Matthew reffed on his hands and knees, before they threw him in juvie, before they threw him in rehab, before they threw him who the fuck knows where. Abel had a sick hit on him—he works at Shell most nights after six—but, back then, on our glass-tattered field, he was almost sub-par at best. LaMarcus threw the ball like a murderer, he'd nail you right in your fucking eye, or maybe that one spot in your knee, or else mid-stride, full speed, just square in the balls; but now that motherfucker's a gardener with this boyfriend out in the Heights. Stefan's a faggot too, only he'd told us right from the jump. Tommy Lee pulled home runs from his ass on the regular, but lately he's been manning this pawnshop with his sister; and the sister, her name was Passion, she actually peeped us from the stands, and we catcalled at her, said give us something to grab at, we dropped our shorts and stuck out our tongues and took the sight of her bugging back home, terrified the whole time, because who knew what she'd do with us; and one day we'd been talking shit on the grass when she grabbed Abel's bat and knocked a pitch square out the block, right through our hands, she ran those bases like a motherfucker, and now she's got a kid with some Vietnamese cat in Bellaire. Demetrius Quinto was no good for catching, and no good for hitting, just trash at movement in general, until one day we had him bunting and he couldn't do that either and now he runs a parlor on the corner of Montrose. Colby could hit, but then he went and got strung out. Donny hit the pipe. Nelly hit it too. Paco held third base, the only Mexican in the neighborhood, we called him Big Mac since his folks held court at McDonald's like seven days a week, and he was the other guy who made it out, got a free ride to Stanford, and then overseas, to make it back a decade later with a PhD and all the clout in the world. Jonathan and Jaycee were reliable benchers, and Juicy was the only brother among them who did time. Ivan did time. Connor did time. Bailey and Raymond and Kool-Ray did time.

There was one night, just after Harvey, and the streets were all the way flooded, and you couldn't run the bases for shit, let alone wade through the dirt, but, even still, we all knew our steps, it felt primal, like birth, like this shit we just knew how to do, and our toes grazed the asphalt and our legs took us through it, and that night Micah rounded the bases like a dog before he finally got his ankle stuck in a pothole by the fence. Dude fell sideways. Like a block of burnt wood. Screaming like I don't know what. So Tommy grabbed his fingers, and Criss-Cross grabbed Tommy, and Dawson held Quinto, and Kendall tugged Dawson. John tagged on to Jaycee, and I grabbed Juicy by his hips, and his Nikes wouldn't budge until Passion grabbed my belt, yanking at my waist, tearing at the seams; and Kool-Aid pulled Passion, and Dawson budged Kool-Aid, and Micah flew out of that hole. You'd think the motherfucker would've thanked us, would've looked us in the eyes, would've at least mumbled something with some semblance of gratitude, but what he did was take off and clear the rest of those bases. Ran through his shoes. His socks. He dove into the mass of us. And we let him do that, we let him take us to the mound. He carried us through the water, and the mud, all the way back home, and that might be why he's the one playing in Brooklyn and Boston and Pittsburgh and Dallas and Tucson and Cleveland and Oakland, but when you catch him on ESPN, or FOX Sports SW, or Telemundo 40, or wherever the fuck, then we're right there with him, holding him up, pushing him toward wherever we're headed next.

FANNIN

Everything is different now, but for a while I lived off of Fannin. Yolanda and I rented this piss-yellow walk-up. It's still behind the fire station, right before the bars. We both worked at the museum downtown; it was my third or fourth job since I'd left the restaurant. One morning we were driving back drunk from the clubs when I saw my father walking up the side of the road.

It was two or three past midnight. We hadn't had any luck at Liberty Station or Julep's. Just the usual goons looking for ass on a Sunday, although it would be a few more years before I stopped looking myself. Yo was driving, and I said, Stop, please stop, and she said, Jan, fuck, you're crazy, just wild, but it's cool, some weekends you win and some weekends you don't, no reason to lower the bar for these niggas. Yo was talking about some other fucking thing, about me not having a man, or having them and losing them, but I didn't care about that, not really. Didn't. Don't. So I reached for the steering wheel, a little fucked-up, a little high, and Yo finally opened her eyes when she realized I was serious, and she stomped on the brakes, and we both sort of flew.

Any further down the road and we would've hit the tracks. Yo's car slowed a bit by Margaritas to Go. She told me to cool it, to calm the fuck down, so I inhaled a bit. Cooled it. Calmed down. I looked back at the man on the road, because of course sometimes people see things. Your eyes will show you what they want to, or whatever they think you should see. They'll show you a happy family when all you have is bodies in a room. They'll show you a man worth walking out on your whole fucking life for, a man who will leave you with three kids and a half-rotting lot, but because your eyes are your eyes and you know what you know, you won't see the train until it finally hits you.

That's him, I said.

Who? said Yo.

My father, I said, and Yo blinked before she laughed.

Yo used to share her apartment with some guy, but then the guy moved out and I filled in the rest of the rent. Most nights we'd hit the Heights, or we'd dance with the gays in Montrose. We'd take shots downtown. We'd strut through the Galleria. No matter where we went, everyone thought we were supposed to be there. The whiteboys I found in Midtown didn't know my brother sold smoke. The Filipinos from the Medical District didn't know my mother couldn't cope. I had an Afghani guy once, his fingers felt like chocolate, for a minute I lived with him in this hotel room on the ninth floor of Zaza, but then his visa went up and he had to fly back home, and he asked to take me with him, actually offered to fly me back, and he didn't know my other brother sucked more dick than the peddlers on Waugh, or that my mother spent whole months crying because of it.

No one knew these things. What I didn't do was tell them. It took me a while to figure out that we're only who we allow ourselves to be.

Eventually I'd marry a whiteboy. A doofy guy who treats me well. We have a kid, an angel, and another one on the way. I say it'll be my last child, but I know he wants another, and I want him to want things. I actually like that. But, at one point in my life, I wouldn't have looked at my husband twice. Or I would have, three times. I would have laughed in his face.

My father had on these tattered khakis. Boots with holes in the heels. I opened the door with Yo screaming her lungs out behind me. He sped up when he saw me coming, then he looked again, and then he was running, but this happened back when I was light, the lightest I'd ever been, no mother, no brothers, no one to hold me back.

I walked my father down and grabbed him by the shoulders.

Hey, I said, pulling at his jacket.

Look at me, I said.

Hey, I said.

My father smelled like trash. He swept at my hands. Filthy hair. Slumped shoulders. His fingers cracked like firewood.

Yo was the only one who knew where I came from. I told her about my brothers, and our home above the kitchen. I'd tell her how Javi essentially ran a brothel out of his bedroom, or how, some nights, my mother woke up just to sit at the dinner table.

Yo would brush her bangs. She'd whistle real low. Say, Weren't you and I lucky to make it out of the crazy?

But, the thing is, it was never really that bad. Or it *was* bad, fucking horrible, and what I did was deal. Some nights, way later, I'd sit on the rooftop of some bar, with Houston's swampy air and a beer, and a brass band playing, and some fuck paying my tab, and I'd think, okay, this is it. This was worth all of that shit. Javi and the rest of them. It happened, but I'm here—and where are they? I could not even tell you. And, believe it or not, these evenings weren't far and few between. They were like mosquitoes. I'd miss them for patches, but not too long. I couldn't get enough.

My father said my name once, and then once again, and then I realized it was Yo pulling at both of my shoulders.

She settled behind me, kneeling on the asphalt. She stared at my father. He looked at me. I looked at Yo, and then the man beneath me, and he blinked at the two of us.

Jesus fuck, he said.

What the shit, he said.

She's sorry, said Yo. She's so fucking sorry.

And I said it, too.

I really tried to mean it.

But I wasn't sorry, because it was my father.

Maybe just for a second. Maybe he was there and then he was gone. But that didn't mean he wasn't there at all.

In the car back home, Yolanda didn't say much about it.

Happens to the best of us, she said, pulling at her hair.

She said, Did I tell you about Lamar?

He had me running in circles, too, said Yo. Chasing niggas into the street.

But one day you just get tired, said Yo. You end up just done with all that.

I don't think I need to tell you that nothing like that ever happened again. We moved out of the piss apartment a few months later. Yo found a new job, and I pulled a promotion at the gallery, and eventually it just became easier to find our own spaces across town.

Now, Yo's gone. In Austin with some man from Malaysia. We talk on the phone from time to time. She asks how I'm doing, if I'm really okay.

A few years later I met my husband at the museum, this other museum, and not because he bought me a drink or pulled my number from a hat. He just showed up. Then he kept on doing that. He bought a ticket every day, and then one day he asked me out. If you'd told me that this could happen to someone like me, I would have called you a liar, but it wouldn't be the first time I've been wrong. I'm still learning. Still picking things up.

When I told my mother we were getting married, she didn't say a thing. She just looked at me for a long, long time.

The next time I saw her, she asked me why I hadn't asked for her approval, and I actually laughed. It was the first time I'd seen her in months. I wasn't in the habit of checking in, and when my younger brother saw us in the kitchen, he scowled.

Figures, said Ma.

I'm not even surprised, she said.

Then she said, At least one of you is doing it right.

She looked me in the face, and said, The thing about slow learners is that they eventually do learn.

And there was a lot in that. Another sentence behind it. Something I knew that, if she told me, I would never forget. But before she could open up and give me whatever it was, the bell dinged down by the restaurant's register, my brother had let someone in, and my mother gave me one last look before she disappeared, and that was it, more or less, the conversation was gone.

WAUGH

Poke lived in a one-bedroom with five boys and a window. The complex sat on Montrose, just across from St. Thomas. They rented it from a woman who couldn't be bothered with a lease, or regular maintenance, or even a deposit; Rod had talked her down so that she wouldn't raise the charges on them. Rod was the one who spent the least time fucking around. He was always out tricking. Most of them were. But, on the rare mornings Poke awoke on the fading carpet of the room, he could watch crowds from the chapel drifting up the block. The apartment sat next to the Chevron on Richmond and the pharmacy on Yoakum, with the diner in between, and Poke would hover by the window, humming at the sink, willing the tap into something a little nicer.

Usually he was cleaning up from last night's john. Poke tried to keep things local. It made life easier. Most guys were fine getting jerked off in their cars, or driving Poke and the other boys a block from the bars on Fairview—but others insisted that they had to be comfortable, and these were the ones who took Poke home with them.

Although, once, Poke ended up at Memorial Hermann. He'd been sucking off some doctor and the doctor was on call. The doc's pager went off, and he wouldn't leave Poke at his place, so he drove him to the hospital and stuck him in the waiting room. Poke sat beside a pair of bleached blondes waiting for painkillers, three bespectacled Mexican women, and some whiteboy with his head in a bandage. The whiteboy looked broken, and he slumped beside his girlfriend, but even through the gauze he was the only one who stared.

When Poke finally asked what'd happened to his face, the whiteboy's girl grabbed her guy by the shoulders.

The whiteboy said he'd been cooking and he poked himself.

Poke smiled, but he didn't laugh.

The other boys Poke lived with were fine: Scratch and Google and Knock and Nacho. They worked the same bars, the same apps, hustled the same set of clubs. They looked out for one another well enough—like when Google'd told Poke about dragging his heels, so he wouldn't track shit from the street into a john's house; or when Nacho'd advised, after staring for months, that Poke find himself a shirt that didn't scream pato.

But it was Rod who'd given Poke his crew's rules of engagement: don't do anything you wouldn't do twice; never, ever, ever double-wrap your rubbers; never give your government name, find some shit that's cool on the ears, and when Poke told Rod that he didn't really get that since his name was his name and it's what he was called, Rod christened Poke as Poke.

That's what got you a regular, Rod said. You established patterns. Patterns became routines. Routines meant a sure buck most days of the month, and that's what kept the lights on.

When Poke asked Rod about his new name, he never got a straight answer. The dude always dodged him. But one day Google told him: it was because Poke was thicker than the rest of them. All of the other boys wore one another's clothes, all Supreme and Adidas and Urban Outfitters and Gap, except for Poke, who Rod made solo purchases for.

Rod wasn't their pimp, but you'd be a fool to tell him that. He took rent from the boys. He bought food from H-E-B. He kept the carpet decent. He scrapped with the whiteboys on Yoakum. He made the rounds at all the shelters for handouts, kept roaches from colonizing the kitchen, and, once, after Nacho'd asked who the fuck made him king, Rod broke his thumbs launching him into the wall.

Poke called a cab to drop them at the Urgent Care on Westheimer. Rod's thumbs swelled like a pair of pale cucumbers. Nacho had a sprained ankle and three bruised ribs, and he wouldn't step straight for the rest of the year. But Rod iced Nacho's ribs. He brought pho from the noodle bar and menudo from the taquería. And although

Nacho still called him el pinche pendejo blanco, there was warmth in those words from there on out. Not respect or gratitude. Nothing akin to praise. Just acknowledgment. An acceptance of the way things were.

It took months for Poke to ask Rod why he'd done that. When Rod answered, it was like he'd been waiting for the question.

Because one day someone's gonna kick the shit out of me, he said. They're gonna beat my fucking ass, and then we'll see what you do.

Rod kept tabs on all his boys, but he kept Poke a little closer. He'd have denied it if you'd asked him, but he felt for the kid—there was something in the way of kinship.

Poke had no history. He'd hit the streets straight out of the shelter. Rod hadn't seen him swapping needles on Almeda, or huffing paint in Hyde Park. This made Poke, Rod figured, a true victim of circumstance. So Rod kept Poke in clean socks. And Rod told Poke which cabbies to dodge. And Rod snuck Poke into Minute Maid Park on an off night during the playoffs, a favor from an ex, and they walked from aisle to aisle palming the backs of every seat, mouthing the names of Astros who'd walked the field before them—Biggio, Oswalt, Peña, and Altuve—muttered like saints under their breath.

One night they sat in Katz's huddled over a Reuben and a milkshake that Rod insisted on despite the extra dollar. Most Thursdays found the boys on Fairview, waiting for the bars to leak their patrons into the morning. But Rod said he had news. Big news. And Poke'd learned not to sleep on an empty stomach.

They rarely ate out, and Poke thought maybe he'd come into some money. It was about fucking time. Maybe he'd found them a bigger spot. Poke envisioned wood floors, painted walls, no rodents, but Rod only sighed, and shut his eyes, and told Poke that he was sick; he'd finally caught the bug.

The two boys eyed each other across the table. Rod with the lighter skin. Poke's a little darker. Rod with the tapered fade, shaved to the neck, and Poke's close-cropped, curly at the top. One a little older, the other a little shorter. Both of them brown in the eyes.

Poke took a long bite from his half of the sandwich. He asked if Rod was sure.

Sure enough, Rod said. The rapid looked sure. Nurse sounded fucking sure.

Okay, Poke said. So take another rapid.

That was the third.

They glanced at the diner door as it yawned open and a gaggle of drunks stumbled in from the cold. Poke blinked through the men, glancing at their ring fingers, wondering how much he could pull. Then he pinched himself.

Rod sipped their shake. He didn't use the straw.

So find a fourth, Poke said, but his voice was cracking.

They didn't know much, but they knew about HIV. They knew the way it hung over Montrose. They took their precautions. And then there was the rule, Rod's rule—you got sick, you were gone. No questions. No exceptions. Your ass was on the street.

And yet, Poke thought.

There was froth all over Rod's lips, strewn with half-chewed pastrami. Poke flicked the end of the straw against his nose.

Fuck, Rod said. What's fucked is I don't even know who it was. I can't even tell you who threw that shit to me.

Poke wanted to say that he'd thrown it to himself—and that's what didn't compute. Not with all Rod's yelling about safety. All the precautions he ran them through. All the grief he gave them. But those words dissolved on Poke's tongue, and he shook his head instead, and he rubbed the nape of his neck with his palms.

Poke started to ask Rod who else he'd told, but he already knew the answer. So he asked when Rod planned to tell everyone else.

Rod took a long sip. He watched the crowd by the window. One of the men laughed, then glanced at their table. He turned away. Then he glanced again.

When Poke reached for the rest of the Reuben, Rod slapped his hand. Soon, he said. I'll figure something out.

Rod stretched in the parking lot, bending toward the high-rises, and the gleam from the streetlamps made his shadow bloom in the night, and the reek of deli meat mingled with the tinge of gasoline, and Poke tightroped the curb alongside the cars congesting Westheimer. It was late. The roads were stuffed.

Rod said he was tired. They should start heading back.

Poke looked at his shoes, kicking at the concrete.

Sure, he said. But it was still only eleven. They had the whole night ahead of them, and when was the last time they'd taken one off?

Rod told Poke that was good and fine. But, really, his night was over.

You're a big boy, though, Rod said. You go on and do your thing.

Just, y'know, Rod said, be safe, and he flashed a grin.

Poke watched Rod saunter away, and then he peeked through the diner's windows. He felt in his pockets for the space where the thread thinned.

Which was how he ended up at Emil's. It was a short walk. The brownstone sat in that patch of grass before the sidewalk dissolved into marsh, littered with bottles and cardboard and dog shit, dampened flyers from the most recent mayoral election. Poke punched the buzzer, and then Emil's voice crackled and the door unlatched itself.

Emil was a furry man. Well into his forties. Curly hair, and his accent was stronger than most. He'd told Poke about his home on the first night they fucked, and how he longed for his family, and Poke'd looked at his skin and rubbed Emil's elbows and tried his best to conjure something in the neighborhood of empathy.

They had a good thing going. Twice a week, most months. Holidays, too, unless Emil was fasting. But as nice as he was, Emil was still a john, and Poke charged him the going rate, or more, when he could swing it.

Except when Emil reached for him now, Poke did a weird thing, something beyond the routine: he hugged the man in front of him.

He did not know he was going to do that until he did it. It was a reaction. An impulse. To what, he didn't know.

They stood in the doorway before an audience of fronds, and the strays patrolling the block, and the dim lights shining through adjacent windows. Poke knew if he'd fucked up, if he'd made a miscalculation, he'd be back out on the curb. He'd have just closed an open door.

But Emil only squeezed him tighter. He told Poke to come in.

Early on, Poke had asked the other boys how they'd found Rod. This was after his shelter years, after he'd made it out from under the overpass. Poke spent those first few weeks in the apartment sprawled across the carpet, watching the other boys come and go, and Rod didn't bitch about it. He said they were glad to have him. He brought greasy sacks from Brothers Tacos, splitting the aluminum evenly across the carpet—but Poke wasn't a fool. He'd seen the other boys eyeing him. He knew he'd have to contribute. He just wanted to know the stakes.

Luckily for Poke, everyone had an answer for him. Before Rod, Nacho'd been another orphan junkie working the Latin bars on Washington. He'd lived in Humble with his aunt and some pocho from El Paso, until they caught him with the poppers. Then he needed a new situation.

He hustled day to day before Rod cut him off at South Beach, snagging Nacho from the lap of some whiteboy by the door. Nacho thought he'd caught a deal—he wasn't green, he'd done this before—but Rod kept tugging, until the man waved them both away.

Nacho called Rod a cunt. He'd lost him that evening's dinner.

Actually, Rod said, I just saved your punkass.

Your boy loves beating on Mexicans, he said, nodding toward the man. What you should be doing is thanking me.

That's when Rod gave Nacho an offer: Stay with him. Work the hot spots across the strip. Maybe slide him a cut of whatever came his way. And, in return, he'd have a place to stay at night, every night, no exceptions.

Clubgoers maneuvered around them. Nacho spat on the road.

He told Rod to go fuck himself.

But still, Nacho told Poke, it's hard. You know? Your boy knew the city. He knew who was carrying real money. I hadn't been downtown too long, so I figured I'd shack up with him for a minute. Cut him loose the next. Maybe case his shit, too. But look. I'm still right the fuck here.

Scratch and Knock met Rod the same way, just talking on the curb. Google found everyone else through Nacho. Rod brought all his boys back to the apartment, this shitty little walk-up in the toe's crack of Waugh, and he schooled them on efficiency, showed them how to get more for their time. Some of the boys took to it, but most of them did not.

There had been others before Poke, but Rod didn't do second chances. A fight got you the boot. A stray needle did, too. One kid, Daisy, woke up looking like a rash, and this other guy, Mick, thought it'd be smart to try tina. Rod let them both go, because he'd told them what was up, the way he told everyone who stepped through his door.

Rod's boys would keep their noses clean. They would keep that shit outside. They would use a fucking condom, or they could pack their shit and bounce. The boys did their best to adhere, for the most part, but occasionally accidents happened, and sometimes rules were overlooked. And, sometimes, Poke found a better way, or a way that was better for him, but if he'd learned anything at all it was that sometimes you kept those things to yourself.

Google was flossing his teeth over the sink when Poke made it back to the apartment. He'd woken up late at Emil's. The blinds had already been drawn. Sunlight fell across Poke on the sofa, cordoned by the fronds tickling the brownstone's windows.

Poke'd snuck out of houses before. He knew how to do it. So before he even opened his eyes he knew it would be futile.

But he tried to anyways. He fished his socks from under the sofa, hooked a sneaker from the kitchen tile, and was scrambling for the other one when he ran into Emil.

Morning!

Hi.

You snore! Emil said. Like a whale!

Emil stood barefoot, in a plaid button-down and slacks.

He held some naan in one hand and Poke's second shoe in the other.

Figured I'd let you sleep, Emil said. Give you a few more hours.

I've got a bed at home, Poke said, and Emil just smiled at that.

Poke said he couldn't stay for breakfast. He had shit to do. Emil nodded at all of this as if he understood exactly. He told Poke he'd drive him home. When the kid declined, Emil called bullshit. Don't think anything of it, no one walks in this weather, it's not the Texan way, ha ha!

It occurred to Poke, dully, as they drifted past the AutoZone and the BBs and the Disco Kroger, that they hadn't had sex after all. He'd spent a perfectly chaste night with a stranger for nothing. Which was a first, he was pretty sure. If not for all the boys, then at least for him.

Emil dropped him off at the walk-up. Poke waved from the stoop. Emil waved back, looking a little sore, and it put Poke's stomach in a knot, as if he was stepping away from something sure, but of course the fucker was still a john.

Now, Google's eyes tracked him across the carpet, from the kitchen to the bathroom to the window and back. Poke washed his face in the sink. What he wanted was a glass of water, but after what had happened to Knock, everyone in the apartment knew not to drink from the tap. It'd put him in bed for a week. Google worked on a bowl of cereal, and didn't say shit about it, which made Poke feel grateful. In fact, Poke didn't mind Google at all—the guy had grown up in Bellaire, in a regular situation, but then his people were deported back to Manila and he'd needed to figure something out.

Long night, Google said, after a while, and Poke nodded.

You're the first one back.

When Poke asked about everyone else, Google only shrugged.

Knock's wherever, he said, and Scratch broke his phone. He's over at Apple. Nacho's with that girl. The one with the ears. Meteor was slow, except for that one guy with the nose ring.

And the eyebrows?

Him.

Fuck.

Fuck's right. You get a cough just looking at him, Google said, and it made Poke think about Rod, and it gave him a slow shudder.

Sure, Poke said, reaching for some cereal, and almost simultaneously Nacho slammed into the room.

Hey, bitches, he said, sneering just a little, and he hadn't even locked the door before Google was cracking the window. Nacho reached in his jeans for a joint, and then he was sealing the paper shut, and the three huddled by the window, inhaling deeply and blowing into the breeze.

The air felt crisp. A trill from some birds spilled across a rooftop. When the smoke blew back, they waved their hands, straining against the wind, and a handful of women powerwalked just below them. They waved at the boys. The boys waved back.

They're living dangerously, Google said, and Nacho hissed, and Poke smoked.

Where hides our lord god the king? Nacho said, and Google nodded toward the bedroom.

Poke blinked twice.

You said everyone was out.

I said everyone that went out was out. Your boy stayed in. Guess he didn't feel so hot.

Something's always wrong with that nigga, Nacho said. He twiddled the joint with his fingers, sucking the smoke a little harder, but even with a wall between them the words came out under his breath.

So no one's checked on him, Poke said.

Why the fuck would they, Nacho said.

He'd call if he was dying, Google said, and Nacho just laughed at that, and Poke brushed at his shirt before he slipped into the bedroom.

The walls were posterless, propless. Peeling at the ceiling. Rod's comforter smelled like peaches, and Poke found him on the mattress, beneath its lone sheet.

He lives, Rod said, raising his arms.

Poke asked how he felt.

Like a bag of Tic Tacs, Rod said.

Good news can do that to you, Poke said, and Rod told him that his news was great.

Poke'd seen sick men under the bridges in Midtown. He'd seen shrunken hands squeezing loose strips of cardboard. Poke knew that everything could and would be fine, until all of a sudden it wasn't.

But today Rod still looked like Rod. Maybe even a little more handsome.

We should find you some treatment, Poke said.

Of course, Rod said. From the doctor. With my insurance.

Don't play dumb, Poke said. You know about the clinics. All the volunteers on Jackson.

And leave you motherfuckers here to run the ship? Rod said. Sure. Great idea.

I'm just saying, Poke said. There's places you can go for free.

And places I will go, Rod said, but it's only been a day.

It's been a day since you found out, Poke said, and he found himself standing. There's no clock on that shit. Maybe you got it from your first fuck.

Easy, Rod said.

Maybe you got it from your ex, Poke said, all up in Rod's corner, leaning over the mattress, hands choking the comforter, and with a speed that made Poke flinch Rod socked the younger dude in the nose.

They stared at each other.

It'd been as simple as flicking a light switch.

Poke saw himself bashing the motherfucker's face in, grinding down with his palms. He'd always thought he could do that, if he really had to. But he knew he never would.

And, Poke thought, at this rate, why would I?

He hated himself for thinking it.

He cut Rod off when he opened his mouth.

Stop, Poke said. I know what you meant. It's fine.

It isn't fine, Rod said.

No, it's all right.

It wasn't fair.

Okay, Poke said, but nothing's fair.

But, said Rod, and then the door exploded behind them, and Knock and Nacho and Google stumbled into the bedroom.

Nacho thought you were fucking, said Google. I told him you weren't.

Lotta noise, said Nacho. Had to confirm.

Sounded like a fight to the death, said Knock.

Of course it did, said Rod.

And then the four of them stared at Poke, and they squinted, and he smiled.

Then Poke touched his nose.

The blood dripped like a leak. It blotted onto his fingers, staining the carpet, seeping into the bottom. Poke rubbed it in with his toes, spreading the liquid thin, and he smiled at the boys.

Everybody inhaled.

Poke fucked around with a number of guys. Some of them were memorable but most of them weren't. He fucked accountants and nurses and gas-station clerks and students. He fucked a guy who couldn't finish unless Poke wore a mask, and another who couldn't finish for anything, not until Poke had spent himself thrice. One time, he left with a woman who'd brought him for her husband, who'd insisted that she stay in the room until they were done.

Worse were the ones who popped the question: could you live with them? The ones who swore they'd take care of you. All you'd have to do was hang around, take a fucking every now and again. Disappear when they needed you to. Reappear just as suddenly. They'd tell you how much they loved you, how they couldn't live without you, and that was Poke's cue, it was all he needed to hear. He rubbed their heads and scratched their chests. He smiled at their jokes. He did all of these things because they'd never see him again.

Rod didn't mention his diagnosis the next week.

That week became a month. Two months eased into three.

Moments to disclose came and went. They popped up in the apartment, as the sky dimmed through the windows, and in the evenings while the boys slunk along the walls of Blur, and under the pulsing bass of Guava Lamp, and, in the morning, piled onto the sofa, after everyone had made it home, and a lull in the conversation had bloomed, and a blip propped open for confession, and Rod would take a deep breath, cross his legs, and brace himself, but what he actually ended up doing was nothing.

He'd spit some sort of aphorism. Ask if his boys were good on cash. Mention something about the cost of electricity, the fact that they were always wasting gas.

It pissed Poke off. All that talk about accountability.

Doing the right thing for your family when you could. And here Rod was—fucking around. Over pride.

So Poke began to press him. He'd wait until they were alone. At the apartment, or on some barstools, or in the booth of some diner.

But whenever Poke brought it up, Rod only shrugged.

I don't know what the fuck you're talking about, he'd say, hardly even dropping his voice.

Rod wasn't delicate about it. The other boys noticed. This brusqueness between them was new to everyone, a chill. They asked and they asked and they asked, and Poke told them it was nothing. Or at least nothing that mattered. That's just how Rod was.

But Rod still tricked, four, five, six times a week. And Poke knew there was something wrong with that. Something irremediably fucked. He never wondered if Rod used protection because he knew that he did not, and Poke tried mouthing the words to himself, just to see what they'd sound like: Our leader has failed us. Worse than the guys he's gotten rid of. More lost than they ever were.

Poke didn't like the way any of that came out.

So some days Poke left the apartment, stepped through the leaves plaguing Montrose, and watched the traffic straddling West Alabama. The garages along the road spat their stew of bachata and country. Poke peeked into the Black Labrador, where people huddled over their gins, and he walked past the library, across Richmond, over I-69, and he watched the cars speed from one end of the Loop to the other.

. . .

A couple weeks later, Poke told Emil.

Poke had found himself at Rod's apartment less and less, popping in only when he absolutely had to. He was spending most of his days on the streets, or lying around at Emil's, though he figured that'd be short-lived. Poke assumed that the man would drop him eventually. He'd tire of this louse with his grime and his sullenness, and his fingers all over the countertop, and his piss all over the toilet bowl. Poke waited, hoping for the worst, but the worst did not come.

Emil never said a word.

Emil washed the dishes. Emil wiped the counters.

Emil left the living room whenever Poke was brooding.

He'd return with a mug of tea. A guest in his own home. The whole thing made Poke burn, made him blush.

So, when he told Emil about Rod, he wanted only to see what would happen.

Emil's lips froze.

He stopped moving. Stopped breathing.

He asked if Poke had it, too. Poke said he did not.

Emil winced, shifting.

I get tested, Poke said. Often.

Often, Emil said.

Every few weeks, Poke said. Last week. And I'm on PrEP.

The pills? You can afford them?

They're free for me.

And then Emil deflated into the recliner.

They lay down in the bedroom. Poke sipped tea from a mug. The sex they'd had was rough, or at least rougher than usual, enough for Poke to feel like he had it in him to say something. And Emil actually apologized. Said he didn't know what'd come over him.

An apologetic john. It made Poke laugh. No one would've believed him, no one would've ever thought it conceivable. And that was enough for Poke to want to try again, and he straddled Emil, rocking the frame until the other man moaned underneath him.

Afterward, they realigned themselves, lost in a bundle of sheets.

Poke'd heard enough of Emil's story by then to write the book on him: Emil fixed computers for a living, or he broke them, or he fixed them to show other folks how to break them, and people paid him to do this. He'd grown up in a country that no longer existed: Emil had lived with his mother, his father. A sister. The mother cared for the children and the father delivered babies, bringing them into the world from a shack on the outskirts of town. He stumbled home every evening with a sack full of vegetables, and sometimes flowers for his wife, and sometimes a treat for Emil. They played games over dinner, guessing which names he'd given that day. His father's favorite, whether for a boy or a girl, was Sasha.

So, Emil said.

There were only so many, said Emil, and my father would cheer every time I got one right. He'd call me a magician. A seer.

As Emil got older, his country's politics grew complicated. A resistance formed within the working class. The government retaliated. Emil's parents didn't want any trouble, they struck an awkward truce with the neighborhood, and Emil watched as their friends began to split among themselves. After someone started a fire in the house next door, his mother kept her children from going outside.

Poke said that must've sucked. Emil assured him it hadn't.

On the contrary, he said, we made our own world indoors. Our house had districts, villages. They had histories and legends.

Emil told Poke that that time was the thing in this life he most missed.

One evening Emil's father came home in the middle of the night, with blood all over his pants, soaked through to his knees. Emil and his sister wailed, but their mother immediately went for the towels in the cupboard. None of them asked where the blood had come from, but soon it was clear that it hadn't belonged to their father.

Emil's mother destroyed the garments. His father never told them what happened. No one in the house ever mentioned it again.

The family left the next morning—they caught a ride with Emil's uncle. Emil told Poke that they drove for days. They passed towns he'd never seen before, smoldering and stricken, and Emil fell asleep and woke up and fell asleep. He was always lulled back under by his mother's low hums, and eventually he heard the cry of planes leaving a runway, and that's when the car finally stopped; they'd reached the country's final checkpoint, and Emil's uncle stopped once a sentry flagged them down.

The boys who pulled them over weren't much older than Emil. They smelled like cigarettes, with rifles slung across their shoulders. Emil imagined his father slipping the straps over their heads, flinging the weapons aside, sending them home to their mothers, and that's when one of the boys told his uncle their car was too full.

For their safety, they'd have to bring it around to the other side of the road.

Emil's uncle sighed. His brother swallowed deeply. Emil's mother gave her husband a slow, sidelong glance.

Emil's father and his uncle stepped from the car, hands in the air. They showed the boys their papers, and the boys simply nodded. They said that the car was too full.

Emil's father told the boys that they weren't leaving their country, they were taking a weekend outing, the airport was simply on the way, and the boys simply nodded. They said that the car was too full.

Emil's uncle, crying now, told the boys that they were doctors, medical professionals, that it was possible he'd brought them into the world, and the boys, if only a little slower, nodded, expressionless, and they asked the men to walk to the curb, they'd only be questioning them for a moment, and Emil's uncle began to sob, slowly, and Emil's father exhaled, deeply, and he blinked slowly at his wife, and he smiled at Emil's sister, and he had finally looked at Emil when the boys shot them both in the back of the head.

The boys stepped around the bodies, firing twice more into both.

The boys looked into the car. They squinted into the backseat.

Emil's sister screamed. He felt as if he were drowning on the air. But his mother wordlessly maneuvered herself into the driver's seat.

She asked if the boys needed anything else.

She said she had the children's papers. She could show them the documents. She unfolded them on the steering wheel, setting them where her husband had sat just before.

They're here, she said.

She told the boys to check them. The boys looked at Emil's mother. They told her she could pass.

They waved to the kids in the backseat, told them to have a nice day.

They arrived in Los Angeles. They moved to Arizona. Emil's mother made her family a life in Phoenix, where she died a few decades later.

Emil's sister lived in Austin. She sent her brother cards. Sometimes she paper-clipped photos of her family, with a smiling boy and a white man in her arms.

So, Emil said. I don't know what your friend should do, he said. I only know what I know. But I know that when you choose, you choose for yourself.

Poke stared at Emil. Then he stood up, and lumbered into the kitchen. He came back with a glass of water, and Emil thanked him with a grin.

Poke allowed Emil to weave his fingers through his hair, and Emil asked him how he'd feel if it were like this every night.

Poke didn't say a damn thing.

He settled into the sheets, crooked his head on Emil's knee.

It was a while before he fell asleep, and his dreams were not unpleasant.

Poke spent the next morning dozing on the sofa. He didn't mention Emil's question, and Emil didn't bring it up. When Emil dropped Poke off, he waved goodbye, and Poke waved back, and he wondered if he'd ever see him again.

Nobody asked Poke where he'd been, or why he'd come back. The boys accepted him wordlessly. Scratch griped about the heat and Google told him to get a job and Knock called them all lazy fucks, and this, Poke thought, was just how life worked.

They took the night off, opting to walk the streets of Montrose. Nacho lifted a couple of six-packs from the CVS. The night felt pregnant with excitement for Poke, as did the next few evenings, and if he felt something missing then it sat under his gut, rustling only in periods of silence.

Poke didn't think about Rod. He didn't think about Emil. He thought about cheeseburgers from M&M Grill and getting fucked up and watching *Your Name* at the theater on Greenway Plaza and the way the flowers on Elgin blossomed beside the town houses.

A few mornings later, Poke was eyeing the apartment ceiling when Google kicked him square in the ass. Wanna hear something wild?

Probably the last thing I need, Poke said.

Too late, Google said. Our humble leader's been taking less calls. I heard he's been turning people away, Google said, and he expected Poke to say something.

But all Poke did was blink.

Bullshit, Poke said.

Real talk.

Really.

You know anything about that?

Poke knew that the moment had fallen square into his lap. It would not come this easily again.

No, Poke said.

Figures, Google said.

The two boys settled into the silence. A pair of drunks argued downstairs.

Who'd you hear that from? Poke said.

People who'd know.

Poke looked at Google. He really didn't mind him. He asked why the fuck Google was telling him now.

Ha, Google said.

Because he's your boy, Google said. Figured if you didn't know, it wasn't happening.

Well, Poke said.

He picked at the hair on his thigh. And, for a moment, it looked like Google would say something devastating, something irreversible, the sort of thing you can never take back. So Poke did a very smart thing, a very sensible thing: he raised his leg, shut his eyes, and let one go.

Fucking animal, Google said, but Poke looked him in the eye and saw that he was grateful.

The next afternoon, Poke was dozing on the sofa, drumming his fingers along the length of his hip, when Scratch called him outside to the porch, practically yelling.

Doesn't matter why, he said. Fucking family meeting.

Poke found the boys smoking in a loose congregation. They passed a cigarette between them.

Why the fuck we gotta whisper when we're out here paying rent, Knock said.

Getting our backs broke for it, too, Scratch said.

Because I said so, Nacho said. Fuck.

Poke, he said. We think your boy's got the bug.

A long horn went off in the lane below. A sliver of Spanish slipped out of an open window. Poke raised his eyebrows very high, and then sent them very low, and he thought about how you only felt so much in your face.

Okay, he said.

Okay, Scratch said.

Word, Google said.

Okay? Nacho said. Okay? You fucking hear me?

Well, Poke said.

Let's say he does, Poke said. Hypothetically.

Hypothetically? Knock said.

Like, let's imagine, Google said.

So Rod might not, Knock said, but he also—

Let this nigga speak, Nacho said.

All I'm saying, Poke said, is if he does have it—and I'm not saying he does—then so fucking what?

The boys looked at one another.

I mean, what's it matter to you? Poke said.

It matters because this motherfucker's lying, Nacho said. It matters that we've got a motherfucking hypocrite in the house. And you know the rules. You fucking know the rules. This shit is not new and you know what needs to happen.

So he's poz, Poke said. Okay. Whatever. But you think you just breathe that shit in? You think it's like a fucking cold?

It isn't, Google said.

Really, Scratch said.

Look, Knock said. We feel where you're coming from. We get you.

He's your buddy, Nacho said. He brought you in. He made you a good boy and he got you off the street. Just like every nigga out here. Did the same for me. I know where you're coming from.

The rest of the boys nodded. They allowed a moment of silence to pass.

But, Poke said.

But we can't have that, Nacho said. We can't have niggas walking around talking shit about us, too. Saying we're sloppy. Because that's what's been happening. That's what niggas are saying. Or hadn't you noticed?

And the truth was that Poke hadn't. He really hadn't known. Between the thing with Emil, and the pocket of tricks he turned regularly, word of mouth and reputation weren't things he'd had to worry about. But, glancing from one boy to the next, he saw this wasn't the case all around. There had been repercussions, even if he hadn't seen them.

So you boot him off the island, Poke said.

That's not what he's saying, Google said.

It is exactly what the fuck I'm saying, Nacho said.

We're all saying it, Knock said.

And you're gonna do it, Nacho said.

Me, Poke said.

You, Scratch said.

Because, Nacho said.

If you're really this motherfucker's friend, Nacho said, if he's really your fuckboy, you don't want me having that conversation.

And, he said, gesturing across the entirety of the porch, you really want anyone else to?

Way back when, the summer after Poke left the shelter, he walked the heart of Houston over the course of a month.

He walked past the palm trees lining the Galleria.

He walked through the smog hanging over Memorial Hermann.

He walked over the concrete sprawl of Reliant, down to the fields overlooking Rice by the park.

Poke sold cheap dope and DVDs. When he could afford it, he bought hash from the Nigerians lining McKinney. He slept on the curb of Washington Avenue as partygoers sidled around him, sloshing beer from plastic cups between the cracks around his head. Poke would dip his finger into the gravel, dab it against his tongue, and decide that he hadn't missed anything much at all.

When winter came around, Poke found himself under a bridge. He didn't have any sheets and he was not the only one. He filched what he could from the yards of the condos lining Alabama, stepping over the Christmas lights, careful not to tangle himself in the bulbs, but once he'd settled behind a column they were always torn off his back.

Some nights the other homeless beat the shit out of him too. Occasionally, although less often, they settled down beside him. But mostly they took what they wanted and left, and Poke watched them go, shivering under the cold, and he saw that, sooner than later, something would have to change.

Eventually, he saved enough money from dealing to pick up a metro pass downtown.

He'd board the rail just before midnight, jumping off once the day workers started to cluster.

Near the end, they were his best customers. They swapped tamales wrapped in foil for whatever movies were under his sweater. Some mornings he fell asleep to the tune of their laughter, and the murmur of the melodies they hummed under their breaths.

Weeks or months later, Poke was dozing on the rail when Rod kicked him awake with the heel of his sneaker.

What Poke did was ignore him. He'd had a long day.

He'd started picking up trash in the park, a job that paid less and less every day. The whitegirl who managed them was a brunette with glasses, she only looked a little older than Poke, and she forked over less than half of his pay. When the workers opened their mouths, she'd told them it wasn't her problem. If they really cared that much, she said, they could get a fucking degree.

Now Poke was tired. He couldn't even meet Rod's stare. The rail driver was too caught up with the tracks to care about the strays in the back.

If something happens, Poke thought, better it happen here, with the camera that may or may not be on to record it.

But what happened was nothing. Rod left him alone. As he stepped off the rail, some women in neon dresses replaced him. They wore glasses shaped like numbers, a little tipsy for the evening. They laughed in each other's arms, and Poke remembered that it was New Year's.

The next night Rod kicked him again.

He nodded at Poke's bag, flushed open with cans. You got diamonds in there, said Rod.

No, said Poke.

Must be something, said Rod, you're holding it so tight.

Poke only nodded. Then he got off at the next stop. It wasn't his usual route, but he hadn't felt like chatting. He hadn't felt much like talking as of late, and even after it began to rain he didn't regret his decision.

Shit had only gotten worse. Poke made even less cash

than before. And the whitegirl in glasses only shook her head in reply.

This must be the jackpot, said Rod, leaning over him, and Poke just shrugged.

By the way, said Rod, you from here? Houston?

Poke looked at Rod. Then, quickly, he shook his head.

Too bad, said Rod. I used to stay in Bellaire. Full house. Wood cabinets and everything.

What happened, said Poke.

Who knows, said Rod. Same thing that always happens. Things changed. I had to go.

Rod had slowly inched his way from his perch near the train door. Today he was wearing a jacket, something Poke knew he couldn't have bought by himself. When Rod caught him staring he squeezed it with a grin.

Zipper's stuck, he said. Beat it off a meter man.

Doesn't matter, said Poke. Still works.

You like a pirate or something, said Rod. An urban scavenger?

Or something.

And how's that working out for you?

It's working, said Poke, and Rod nodded in agreement.

Fair enough, said Rod. Gotta take what you can get.

They watched the city through their window, flanking the corner of the Medical District. They rode past the churches, up Buffalo Bayou Drive, until they plowed across the Galleria's sprawl beside the Village. When the doors slid open, neither boy made a motion to move. The conductor eyed them in the back, pulling a cigarette from her purse.

You can keep on, she said, but not for free.

Poke neither moved nor breathed when Rod skipped down to pay for another loop.

They heard the whoosh of the doors as the rail rose again. They kept not speaking as the city glided beneath them.

The next time Poke showed up at Emil's, he brought a bag that he'd stuffed with all of his shit.

Emil didn't mention it. He extended his hand. He ushered Poke in, showed him where to drop his clothes, and Poke did his best not to think about Rod's new situation.

Emil explained about the locks in the apartment. He showed Poke how to fold the sheets. Poke learned that the water from Emil's tap was drinkable, that he didn't have to boil it or disinfect it or anything, and it was this discovery that nearly sank him, crumpling him into a heap by the cupboard.

In the third week, Poke got comfortable. He found himself sleeping in, until nine, ten, eleven. He'd open his eyes to the depression on the other side of the mattress, blinking at the lamps atop the dresser, and, on occasion, he'd wonder about the guys on Waugh. But that only led to thinking about Rod, so Poke rejected the notion entirely.

Emil worked most days. In the evenings, he returned with dinner. He brought home whole roasted chickens, salmon wrapped in bay leaves, tomatoes ripe to the touch. For the first time in his life, Poke looked forward to food. Rice and beans and fish and curry and pasta and pizza and shrimp chips. Eventually, at Emil's insistence, he tried a smear of tzatziki from Aladdin's, and refused to eat anything without it for days.

Emil watched him eat, sometimes talking endlessly. But sometimes he didn't say a word.

Sometimes he just watched.

Most nights they fucked and then other nights they didn't. The new life took getting used to, but Poke'd gotten used to things before.

He'd been living with Emil for a month when he finally asked for the favor. They were sitting at the table, hunched over a bowl of salad. At this point, they'd woven a routine into the evenings, and Poke felt as much a part of Emil's life as anything else.

Poke told him he had a friend. Someone who needed a place to crash.

Not for long, he said. Just to get his feet back under him.

Emil chewed slowly. Poke'd grown used to the hair on his face, and the way that his cheeks rounded out around his nose, and the light in his eyes when he sulked. In all of Poke's time at the brownstone, he hadn't asked Emil for anything. But, then again, he hadn't had to. That hadn't been a problem at all.

Just for a while, Poke said.

A day or two, Poke said. Three max.

Sure, Emil said.

I don't see why not, Emil said, and Poke felt his calves unclench.

The moisture in the room seemed to evaporate all at once. Poke was aware of the clashing colors on the wall. Emil asked him if he wanted more salad, and he nodded, dully, but giddy all the same.

Poke didn't know where he'd find Rod, exactly, but he had a general idea. He hit the soup kitchens on Dowling, and the servers shook their heads. He checked the churches on West Alabama, and the parishioners turned up their noses.

He checked the shelter on Rusk and the shelter on Main and the shelter on Dallas and the shelter on Dunlavy, and the receptionists told Poke that they'd found him, Rod was here, Poke was just in time, he could come right this way, but, when they showed Poke whom they meant, it was just some starving dude they'd pulled off the corner downtown. Poke thought about checking in with the health center on California, or the one on Branard, or this other one across town, but he decided against all that—help was the last thing Rod was looking for. He had too much hubris. That was the reason Poke was out here searching for him in the first place.

So Poke decided he'd ride the metro until he ran Rod down, because their city may have been big, but their orbits were infinitesimally small. He alternated routes. Switched up his plans. He seldom took a day off, seldom broke for midmorning traffic. Poke thought about reaching out to the boys, plugging Google or Knock for a lead, but he knew exactly how that would go.

About a month after he'd started searching in earnest, Poke saw Rod as he glanced through a window by the warehouse district.

He'd nearly missed him. The metro had stopped at a light and Poke got off. Rod was standing in line outside the soup kitchen, leaning like a dwarf among giants. He wore an unfamiliar expression, something Poke couldn't quite put his finger on, and then he realized the look wasn't new or unfamiliar at all, he'd just never seen it on Rod's face.

Poke went over and tugged Rod's sleeve. Rod didn't turn around.

The line shuffled behind them. Rod's shoulders sank. For the first time in a long time, the stench made Poke's skin crawl.

Rod, Poke said, tugging at his sleeve.

Rod, Poke said, nudging his elbow.

John, Poke said, and this time Rod flinched, and he glanced Poke's way, and he did not smile.

Poke waited for Rod to pull his meal from the kitchen. They found a cluster of stone bricks a block from the building. Men huddled on the lumps of moldy sofas around them, donning blankets and scarves and jackets.

Poke looked away. He wore khakis and a cardigan. For the very first time, he thought he really might have moved on.

He watched Rod eat in silence. They stared at the warehouses painted with graffiti.

You got fatter, Rod said, once the sky began to dim. Not that it's the worst thing. You could argue that fatter's good. Fat shows upward mobility. Fat means progress. Growth.

Poke watched Rod chew. He pulled at his sleeves.

How long you been out here, Poke said.

Long enough, Rod said. There was a coup, although I guess you already knew that.

Poke blinked, blushing.

For the first time since Poke'd found him, Rod smiled.

They caught me on a bad day, he said.

And you let them? Poke said.

I didn't let anyone do shit, Rod said. I beat their asses. Then I bounced.

A handful of black dudes in snapbacks walked between them, grumbling. Rod and Poke ignored them.

They took everything, Rod said. All the money. All my clothes. They took my shit and they locked me out. Rod flicked his fingers across his nose. But enough about me. I must be boring you. Don't ask me how I know, but it looks like you've found yourself a sugar daddy.

I want you to come with me, Poke said.

Of course you do, Rod said. You came all the way down here to save me.

Fuck you, Poke said. Emil said he's fine with taking you in.

Jesusfuckingchrist, Rod said, you've moved in. He's got

you calling him by his fucking name. Here I was thinking you'd started your own crew. Running the streets. Paving your way. Never thought you'd turned bitch.

Rod, Poke said.

Full bitch.

I'm trying to help you.

And who's Emil anyways, Rod said. The dust bunny? Terrible fuck.

Poke stood and looked at Rod. Poke jammed his hands in his pockets, flexing his fingers, unforming fists.

He allowed himself to think that his friend looked a little pitiful.

Look at me, Poke said.

Rod didn't.

And then he did.

I'm not going with you, Rod said. I'm not going anywhere. Call it a favor.

Because let's say I steal your thunder, he said. Let's say your plug takes me in. Then what? We both just live with him forever? I mean, imagine I decide to get comfortable. Let's say he asks me to leave. You think I'm just supposed to go? You really think I'd let that happen? You think I'd just leave that shit in peace?

It was something that Poke had considered, Rod's coming in and disrupting everything. Of course it was a possibility. But Poke hadn't allowed himself to linger on it.

No, Rod said. I appreciate your concern. But I'm fine right here. I'll figure something out. And besides, you had your fucking chance. If you wanted to help, you should've stuck around.

Poke stared at the buildings in front of them, and then at the bodies and the trash and the litter. The homeless picked from one another's bundles. A handful smoked cigarettes. Some sat off by themselves, lecturing invisible audiences, and Poke gave them one last glance before he spat between Rod's eyes.

Rod didn't move.

He just took it, smiling.

Poke walked the other way. He turned around to look at his friend. He ran a hand over his face and then he got the fuck out of there.

A couple times a week, Poke used Emil's card and caught a Lyft to the warehouse district. Some days he posted up just across the road. He found a spot beyond the dumpsters, or the fences shielding Clinton, or the shacks stacked west of Hamilton and the feeder beneath the highway. Other days, he crossed the boulevard, staking out a position just beyond view. Far enough to hide but close enough to see.

The days Poke found Rod, he observed him. He lingered. Rod didn't look any worse. He'd become part of the scenery.

Some days, he looked like the Rod who'd taken Poke in. Shining with a stride. The captain of his space.

Most days he did not. Most days he just looked lost.

But Poke watched him regardless. Rod stared as if he were waiting for something. This thing he'd been cheated out of, his end of the deal. And Poke never closed the distance, he never called Rod's name, but he kept coming, and watching, and waiting, for something.

Then one day Poke caught a ride in the afternoon. It'd rained softly all morning. There'd been an accident on the bridge, and a mist settled between the alleys, and Poke's Lyft settled at the light before the intersection, and when he finally looked up he saw that Rod wasn't under the bridge.

He was nowhere to be found.

So Poke checked the city's shelters.

He checked the kitchens and the clinics.

He asked the squatters and the day workers and the addicts he passed on the road. Poke rode through East End and Midtown and Downtown and Montrose for weeks and weeks, scanning alleys and corners and shacks.

He looked for a long time.

ELGIN

1.

Once, I slept with a boy. Big and black and fuzzy all over. We met the way you meet anyone out in the world and I brought him back to Ma's. He saw the candles by the stairs and the lighters on the counter and the boxes in the kitchen and the cans lining the tile, and when he asked if I was coming or going I said this was just how some people lived.

East End in the evening is a bottle of noise, with the strays scaling the fences and the viejos garbling on porches, and their wives talking shit in their kitchens on Wayland, sucking up all the air, swallowing everyone's voices whole, bubbling under the bass booming halfway down Dowling. But with the blancos moving in the whole block's a little quieter now. You've got these dinnertime voices leaking in through the windows. You hear dishes clinking just like in the commercials. It all feels impossible to me, this shit no one I know could afford, but Ma called it cyclical. She said you have things and then you don't.

It's why she had to get out of town, back to Shreveport

with the rest of her people. She swore that Harvey was a sign. Just one more thing that went wrong. The water blew away our porch, swept away all of the gravel and most of the cars, and we didn't even get the worst of it. We could walk our roads a few days later. Jan's neighborhood sat underwater for a week. But whenever I brought up Ma's logic, to tell her things would come back around, she told me niggas don't get to choose.

So she left me in Houston with the house and its new silence.

I fill it with sucios and güeros and hondureños.

And the chinos living down Preston.

And the Nigerians holed up on Cullen.

We both know it's happening, but she won't say shit about it since Ma's man is gone and her daughter could care less and her other son's in the ground.

At some point, niggas have to take what they can get. Ma used to say that too.

When the boy finally comes, it's like he's been shot.

Afterwards, we deflate. Roll to opposite ends.

I tell him not to get too comfortable. Niggas swear they didn't know they couldn't stay if you don't tell them. They'll think they can stay if you don't make it clear they can't. Or they'll scurry out in the morning on Very Important Business: they've got The Job or The Bills or The Deal. The Novia. Every now and again someone actually brings up a baby or a girlfriend.

Once, I fucked this whiteboy whose papi owns like half

the city. He told me to come back to Galveston with him, that all I'd ever have to do is clean and screw.

Once, I fucked this poblano from Guerrero. He was looking for his brother, their coyote had dumped them, and now he was just biding his time in Houston, waiting.

Mostly that's how it goes. A half-story, and they're out. I don't know what happens to these people or where the hell they end up afterwards.

So with this one, I smile. Roll a hand through his hair. He's got these scars flaking up his neck like a sure thing gone wrong.

When I ask where they came from, he hums me away.

I lost a scrap, he says.

You mean you got your fucking head cut.

Whatever, he says, and then he's humming again, and then he's scratching my ear like he cares after all.

2.

We had a few months left in the house when Ma started talking about Louisiana.

We weren't as broke as some of these niggas but we stayed on the edge. Ma lived off soup. I ate at the job. Used to catch the bus at five to work this breakfast gig on Navigation, but after a half-life of flipping tortillas I scored another one out in Montrose. It's this restaurant called the Castillo. I wait tables for Houston's glitterati. I give them something to laugh at over flautas and mezcal.

Ma spent most days indoors. Confined her drifting to the porch and the yard. So when she brought up packing her life in some boxes, and pushing those boxes out of Houston, I told her she wasn't serious, she wouldn't last two minutes on the road.

Except Ma wasn't bugging. And she did last. Her sisters loaded her up to push her right back down I-10.

Ma's people stayed away when Javi, Jan, and I were coming up. They never got down with her husband. They're all dark like Ma, like rust on the rim of the stove, and my father'd called them brutos and said the pack of them could fuck themselves, and that was enough for Ma at the time but then he split and it wasn't.

During Rita, she spent the whole night on the phone. Whispering and crying. Wondering if her sisters had really stopped giving a shit. When Javi saw her huddled up, he slammed the receiver across the room, and it was another year before we got around to finding the cash to replace it.

The only other time I saw them was the night of Javi's funeral. I don't know how they found us. Ma'd told like seventy-two people, but twelve actually showed for the service. My aunts took the aisle behind us. This pastor stood by the windows, and he kept fucking up our names, and two niggas in the back bounced halfway through when they figured out it wasn't their Javi.

3.

Later on, I tell one of the other waiters, Miguel, about nailing the boy. He's wiping the same dish in the back of the restaurant, icing his table out front. It isn't like our blancos don't tip—they do it to keep up appearances, the Castillo's where they come to flex—so we take our time in the rear of the house. We hold their plates until the chills creep in.

Was it good? asks Miguel, and I say the boy was regular. My usual hijo de papi.

Everyone's somebody's son, he says.

Some sons give it better than others.

Except you don't take, says Miguel, and he's starting in on some other shit when one of our cooks slams the door, cheesing like he's already off and tipping dancers at Treasures. Teeth all yellow and busted. Spitting some dark shit in Spanish. But Miguel plays along, laughing, then rolling his eyes when the motherfucker's gone.

Historia de mi pinche vida, he says.

Miguel is obviously a pato. Skinny and crooked and brown as bark. On a bad day he'll talk like he's holier than thou, enough that you have to stuff a rag in his mouth. He crossed with his parents once his sister got sick, back when they were still offing doctors in Guate, and Miguel says his father chose Houston for the hospitals. Because they help invisible folk here. Didn't matter that they were undocumented. But then the sister died and they'd blown all their cash and now they were stuck on this side of the gulf. And they still hadn't tried to pick up some papers, since of course they didn't have the money to leave anyways. To start over? From nothing? Better to make a quiet life in Houston's crevices.

Dude keeps quiet about the whole thing. Works doubles most nights. More when he can swing it. Says he eventually wants to stick his people on a plane back home; Miguel's family's the only thing he ever really spends any scratch on, and the one time I asked how he felt about that he said there was a lesson: don't get sick.

Whenever I'm seating the older blancos, I give him a heads-up. They're generous with us young guys, shaking our hands and squeezing our hips. They know nothing's about to happen. But they still throw change our way, and we don't throw it back, and one time I seated this nigga who said he wished all his boys talked like me.

This other time I had a table by the door dropping c-notes, this gaggle of fags flapping wings in tuxedos. One of the husbands wanted a candle from the chandeliers up close to the ceiling, and his boy tossed me a bill. He told me to go figure it out.

So when Miguel signals me from the bar, I figure he's looking out. But all he does is cross his arms like he's just so disappointed.

I've been thinking, he says.

Better if you don't.

You keep pulling game like that, he says, you're gonna strike out.

Like what?

Like hoods off the street, says Miguel. Like whatever puto feels like poking his head out.

You don't think I'm safe, I ask. Out here? With these niggas?

I'm not talking about that, he says. I just don't think you're bulletproof.

I dodge bullets. That's all fucking I do.

Sure, says Miguel, shaking his head. But that's not what I'm saying.

You're gonna screw yourself up, he says, and he pokes me in my chest.

If anyone else had done it I'd have knocked their fucking nose off. I would've lost my fucking job.

But Miguel has this look on his face.

So I shrug. Squeeze his shoulder. I slug him in the other one, hard.

4.

The nights I'm not lurking I spend back in East End.

With Ma gone, the house is an album. A literal Greatest Hits.

Here's where Javi got bopped for talking big.

Here's where I took my first steps and busted my ass.

Here's where Javi taught me how to box, where he told me I'd never be anything, where he swore I'd end up in the tent city behind Leeland with the Jesus Freaks and cabrones struck by maldiciones.

Most of my fucks know I live here alone. It's usually their first time east of I-90. Between the chop shops and busted laundromats and abuelas like scarecrows on every corner, there's no reason to stick around unless you're a kid. Or you're broke. Or you got stuck like Ma. But one time I brought this guy back, this Peter Parker type from downtown, and he wanted to tour the block after the storm. Had his DSLR and everything, snapping all of the derelict houses. He asked why they still hadn't been rebuilt, and I told him they were like that before we'd even heard of Harvey.

We fucked in the kitchen. I walked him down Leeland. It'd just stopped raining. Four thousand percent humidity. Some kids kicked a ball in the middle of the road while a gaggle of hoods posted up by a Cadillac. Ever since the new mayor, our block's been mostly immune to that gang shit, but niggas knew that they still had to put in appearances.

They kept their eyes on us the whole way down. When I nodded, one pendejo literally spat on the concrete.

My whiteboy kept mouthing Wow.

Wow wow wow wow wow.

He told me I was lucky, I was living in a piece of history, and I said if I was so fucking blessed he should've grown up here himself.

5.

Every now and again I catch one of my boys at the Castillo. Doesn't happen often, but it's happened before. They come through in the morning, brunching in tables of four, and a few nod my way but mostly you'd think I was ghosting.

It's trickier in the evenings. They're either working or with the fam. I do my best to stay out the way but you know how that shit goes. And when it happens tonight with this whiteboy, stuffed between two shmucks in a bow tie—blond and pale and heavy, he'd cried when he popped—the puto actually signals our manager from his post by the bar.

The manager is this guy, Diego, a Salvadoran with an invisible accent. He stands with my whiteboy for a solid minute, until he finally waves Miguel from across the room.

I don't have time for it. I hide out in the back. The Castillo's all business out front, all flash and new money, but the walls beyond the bar are flimsy as fuck. Stepping through the kitchen you cross border after border.

The cooks are huddled around a TV. Some busted box from the nineties. Soccer's on and everyone's tossed their change onto the table.

No matter where you put them, niggas hold on to their vices. Thousands of miles, a whole new climate, and a language away from home, but here they were, dropping scratch for a ball in the grass of some mold-smothered stadium.

I've just caught the announcer's cadence when Diego yells my name.

He's nearly purple. His whole fucking face.

He asks what the fuck just happened.

Must've been an accident, I say.

It's the angriest I've seen him, but I know it'll pass. Diego's used to worse. He grew up in San Miguel. Dude didn't come from money, and he's worked the Castillo for like five years, but he only pulled the top job after the owner's son OD'd in Midtown. Happened at this glitzy whiteboy bar, and no one knew the story for days, but I heard it after Miguel heard it from this kid he'd been seeing at Rice.

After he's torn my asshole open, Diego sighs. Shakes his head. Says he didn't mean to pop, it's just that our guests expect better, you know?

I tell him I do.

He kneads my shoulder. Right after I flinch, Diego says he only wants what's best for everyone.

In the parking lot after closing, Miguel is beaming. The blanquito de chingao tipped him a pair of twenties. It's another addition to the black hole of his parents' travel fund, and I congratulate him for it, and he tells me not to be an ass.

Maybe I'm not fucking with you, I say.

All you do is fuck with people, says Miguel. Like that whiteboy, he says.

So you say.

So you told me.

Obviously it worked out for you.

Miguel shrugs. He's glowing a little, fists stuffed in his pockets. Even this late, the heat's got us both squinting.

It's how you cope, he says.

You think I'm depressed.

I think you screw out your problems, says Miguel. Sí.

Sounds like you're jealous.

Joking won't make it better, says Miguel, and he tugs at the end of his belt.

What's even keeping you here, he asks. In this fucking fishbowl city.

It's actually a bayou.

Mierde, you know what I mean, says Miguel. You told me your mami's left you. It's not like you're waiting on fam. You can't stand anyone for longer than a fuck so I know that's not what's keeping you around. I think you're scared.

You don't know shit, I say.

Also, I say, why the fuck do you even care?

Calm down, says Miguel. You sound like the fucking gringas. All I'm saying's that you can do better. People leave every day.

But you're still here, I say, and it's like I've just kneed him in the balls. Like I've kicked a goddam newborn.

Some whitelady in heels tiptoes around us. She's skipping through the lot with her valet in tow. Leaning all over the nigga like he's a fucking life jacket, and he's eating it up, but it's not like I can blame him.

Yo, I say, after they've passed. Sorry.

Don't be, says Miguel. You didn't bring them here.

I mean I was wrong.

You're not wrong.

That wasn't fair.

Nothing is fair.

The back door cracks open. We get a cheer from the kitchen. Probably from the huevons bullshitting around the game. But Miguel slumps in the light, and the glow is gone, and I feel like I should say something, and I know the moment's passing, but then the door shuts and the epiphany's gone and we're stuck facing Montrose in the dark on the curb.

6.

Houston is molting. The city sheds all over the concrete. We've got bike shares in the Third Ward, motherfucking coffee shops way out on Griggs. We've got like four different shacks with niggas hawking tacos, right next to this barber charging sixty for a trim. The white folks cleared out the garden Miss Contreras set her herbs in—she's got three sons but they're all away: two in jail, one nigga at Princeton—and they dug up the tomatoes and cemented over the seeds and now you've got these trucks selling duck foot sandwiches on potato bread. But after the storm, they pushed the rest of us out, too: if you couldn't afford to rebuild, then you had to go. If you broke the bank rebuilding, then you couldn't stay. If you couldn't afford to leave, and you couldn't afford to fix your life, then what you had to do was watch the neighborhood grow further away from you.

The Hernandez twins are gone. Tatiana's son is gone. Larissa is gone, Santiago is gone, the Garcias are gone, and the Pham family, too. Then there's Griselda's place, this dance studio she runs with her moms. But instead of selling, or letting someone come in and flip it, she lets yuppies from wherever host their yoga in the back. She's in there every morning, checking them in, and every other night she's posted up to kick them out.

Sometimes I'll drop in to talk shit. I'll catch her hunched over, staring at nothing, pissed.

7.

A few nights later, Miguel is beaming. Dude's got a bruise smearing his whole left eye.

I don't ask.

The Castillo's at half-capacity, but Diego's still buzzing around. We're hosting a big to-do soon. Some circle-jerk conference. Diego says that every day, *every day,* is a rehearsal for the larger picture, because we are cementing our reputation, which is to say *his* legacy. You practice how you play. When one of the cooks announces that he hasn't gotten play in decades, Diego breaks character, tells him broke niggas have all day to fuck.

So we're smoothing our ties when I corner Miguel. I tell him it's subtle, whatever he's got going on with his face.

He doesn't laugh or bitch or crack on me.

He says he'll explain over drinks.

I ask who the fuck has money for those.

And also, I say, since when does the son of god get fucked up.

Don't worry about it, says Miguel.

I'm not asking for me, I say. You're the one who's saving up.

Sometimes beggars strike gold, he says, and I'm about to press him when Diego finds us.

He's fanning his face, pointing at an overstuffed table of blancos, like, What the fuck are you doing? He tells me I've been pushing it lately, that I should get my shit together, and he's winding up for more but then Miguel grabs his elbow.

He says we're just clearing receipts. It's been a long day. I was helping him tally his tips.

Of course Diego doesn't buy it. But he grabs Miguel's hand anyways. He squeezes it for a beat.

Then he looks at me and says, So what the fuck are you still doing here.

Miguel drives a Peugeot. It's busted as fuck. His father scored the thing to ferry the family around the city. You can hear popcorn cooking once he flips the ignition, and the tires feel like they're rolling on air, but once we actually start moving the engine gives a little shudder and we're cruising down Montrose, past Alabama, toward Elgin.

The bar isn't far. It's this shack with some benches. Miguel's friendly with the owner, a black lady in an apron. The place is all local, all browns and tans, and when Miguel takes his seat he's got a couple of Shiners already in hand.

He says he's bought two plane tickets. Didn't think it would happen but then it did.

They fly back in a week, he says. Two stops.

One connection in Miami, he says, then they're back in the capital by midnight.

Wow, I say.

I hope you found some decent seats, I say.

Puto, says Miguel.

Then he sighs.

They're going back home, he says.

We take long sips from our bottles.

Felicidades, I say.

When I ask how he pulled it off, Miguel only shrugs.

Opportunity, he says, and I remember his viejos on the side.

Los papis must have paid you well.

I didn't complain.

The sun settles into a muddy purple. It's still hot as shit. But not entirely unbearable. Some crows fly overhead. The road behind us is full of fronds, shading the porches and the yards and their cars, and when I reach for the fresh bruise sitting under Miguel's eye, he jumps before he softens.

It feels a little shallow. A little smooth around the edges.

You cleaned this? I ask.

Cálmate, he says. We're celebrating.

Niggas lose their eyes for less.

Drink with me. That's what we're doing.

I tell Miguel we'll get faded later, that there will never not be time to get trashed, and before he can protest I'm jogging to the pharmacy across the street.

When the doors slide open, there's a pregnant lady behind the counter. She's got this little girl in dreadlocks pulling on the back of her jeans.

I ask where the alcohol is, and she eyes me, and then my uniform, and for a second I think she'll smile but she says, Nigga you ain't even looked.

I make it back with swabs.

Miguel doesn't bitch. He sulks on the curb, flinching, but he still lets me work.

Once we're drinking again, he says, You don't suck at that.

My brother showed me how.

He must've been better.

It was his job, I say, and when I'm done I toss the bottle. It clatters on the concrete, adding rubble to the pile.

Let me guess, says Miguel, your brother's a vet.

Javi's an Army medic. Or he was. Now he's dead.

We don't look at each other. We sit and watch the action on Elgin. Miguel downs his Shiner and tosses that too and we pass the last one back and forth.

Hey, says Miguel.

Qué, I say.

Tell me something about you I don't already know.

You're fucking with me.

I look him in the face to see if he's for real.

Anything, says Miguel.

Shit, I say.

You sort of remind me of this kid I knew, I say. Back when I was little.

Weird, says Miguel.

Yeah. He lived next door. Got evicted and everything.

You remember his name?

No, I say.

Right, says Miguel.

Then he laughs.

You were probably in love with that motherfucker, he says.

I tell him I wasn't but Miguel waves that off. He drops his chin onto his knees.

We drink and watch the street. The streetlamps bring it to life. There's a homeless guy loitering in front of the CVS, and I know offering him a sip would make his whole fucking night. But of course we don't do that, we watch him stalk the road, and once he reaches the island of grass in the street he lies down and shuts his eyes.

8.

My place is smack in the middle of East End, behind the construction and the stadium and a fuckton of traffic. Nearly everyone else's already sold their property and moved on. Life's just cheaper in Pearland and Baytown. After Señor Cortez gave in, it was Esmeralda from the corner, and then Jaime and his brothers, these Nicaraguans always scowling at everything. Then Nikeeta sold her place. Francisco's fam left their house. Joanna held out in her little blue stucco place but the price turned right and she bounced.

Now these blancos live in her house. Our neighborhood's

first white people in fuck knows how long. The whole block's made a show of ignoring them and a couple of hoods took a dump on their Civic. But all I ever saw those motherfuckers do is smile, always waving my way like we came up together, and they had this kid, this little fucking boy, and one time he kicked me a ball, on some nothing day in the summer, and before I knew what was happening I was kicking it back, just me and this kid and his mom by the window, and for a second it was nice but after a minute I took off because there's only so much of that shit that can make sense at one time.

9.

Next time I see Miguel I just look at his face and it's obvious something is wrong.

We're rolling out for a gala. The Castillo's buzzing with money. We've thrown sequins on the windows and glitter all over the floor. The dinner floor's packed, standing room only, and Miguel drops like four plates at the feet of some suit.

He flubs his tickets. He mixes up orders. Another waiter, this prick named Raúl, says he thought patos were good with their hands, and Miguel meets him head-on, he calls him a stupid fucking huevón.

I'm neck-deep in my own shit but I manage to grab his collar.

I ask if he's good. He gives me this look. Then he swallows whatever's in his mouth and says, Claro.

. . .

But of course he isn't.

Shit only gets worse.

Later that night, he's yelling at a table of blancas, these blow-dried mannequin types just about drowning under their pearls, and Diego comes out of nowhere all decked down in a suit. Hair slicked back. Smelling like soap. He tugs Miguel's arm, and I'm reading their lips when this güero snaps his fingers in my face for more salsa.

So I'm still in the kitchen when the fight breaks out.

I don't see who starts it but honestly who gives a shit. Miguel starts throwing hands. Diego covers his face. Miguel socks him in the chin and Diego's just holding on, and you'd think the crowd would explode or cry out but they just circle up with the rest of us to watch.

I don't know if it's the thought of the cash he's losing or the Salvadoran in him or what, but eventually Diego manages to set his feet. He flips Miguel on his back. Puts his knees on his chest, and his hands on his neck, and if he were anybody else it'd be a wrap.

But he just looks down at Miguel.

Diego wipes his mouth. Spits on the tile.

Javi'd call it a pato scramble. There's money at these tables so now everyone's standing, wives clutching their pearls. Some niggas start muttering, and a handful of people head for the doors, but mostly everyone's still watching to see what's gonna happen next.

What Miguel does is stand. He doesn't look up or anything. He turns around, heads for the door, and Diego shouts after him until he's gone.

You'd think he'd have gone straight home or whatever but I find him on the patio. Sitting, shaking his head. Looking like garbage.

Believe it or not the evening hadn't gone completely to shit. Some people left, but most of them stayed, and Diego came out of the kitchen stronger than ever after cleaning himself up. Wasn't flustered or anything, talking all polite to everyone, and when I asked about the tables that bounced without paying, he just shrugged and said, Es en los manos de dios.

Now he's sent everyone home. Gave a big speech about What a great job. That was all some niggas needed, he said Good and they were out, but the rest of us stood around looking lost before we started putting shit back together.

The black outside turns blacker. Drunks start ambling up the road. Miguel keeps his eyes shut, and I don't say shit either, but then he sighs and tells me they're gone.

His folks flew out the night before.

They should be back in the capital by now, he says.

Jesus shit, I say.

So you go full lucha fucking libre, I say.

No, says Miguel.

One of our waitresses finds us on the steps. She asks if everything's all right and I tell her all's well in the jungle.

She looks at Miguel, and then at me, and says, Better out here than in there.

Miguel kneads his eyes, the most tired I've ever seen him.

They asked me to come too, says Miguel.

I had the money, he says, and he just shakes his head. I had the money and I didn't go. I sent them back on their own.

You still have the cash, I say, you can probably leave tomorrow, but as soon as the words leave my mouth I know that's not why he's stayed.

We sit on the curb a little longer. The street cleaners come through. They wait until the city's at its most quiet, right before the first patch of dawn, and they walk from Dallas to Hamilton sweeping at all of the concrete under them. Shit's actually pretty beautiful if you think about it—all the convicts and baseheads and fuckups giving the city a clean slate—but before I tell Miguel he's already fallen asleep. Dude's on my shoulder, arms crossed like he's deliberating.

A gaggle of cleaners passes, smoothing their route around the car. One of them looks over and waves so I give him one back.

10.

Ma spent the first week we sold the house in bed. She didn't care how much we were pulling from the sale. She hadn't grown up in the place, and of course it'd kicked her ass, but even if it's a bag of shit everyone wants their name on something.

My mother, who'd danced with Mexicans. Who'd kicked a pack of hoods from her bar, told them to roost on some other stoop.

Before she took off to Shreveport, I told her she was running from nothing to nothing.

She made this face like she wanted to believe me. Then she said it wasn't like I'd given her any reasons to stay.

Me.

You, she said. You're as rootless as I am.

Ma'd brought it up before—she'd stick around if I started a family.

What, I said.

Jan's got a whole nest, I said.

You've got grandchildren, I said. A son-in-law, too.

It's different, said Ma.

That's bullshit. You're bugging.

Quiet, said Ma.

Look, said Ma.

A daughter who loves you is one thing, she said. Give me the family that wants me around.

She used to ask me about women. When was I bringing one home. Javi had the opposite problem, she said, that boy had Rebecca here and Katrina there. Ma swore my plan was to wait until she rolled over and died, but Javi always told her that I wasn't the one for that.

She'd shush him. Take a deep breath. Say that plums only ripen with time.

Except one day she just stopped. It just wasn't something that came up anymore. I tried chancing it once and Ma said maybe Jan will kick out another one too.

11.

I don't see Miguel the next night. Or the next few nights after that.

I don't seek him out.

I know how it feels when shit happens. I know about needing time.

Back at the Castillo, one of the cooks asks where my boyfriend's gone.

I tell him Miguel is in his bed, fucking his wife and daughters.

The rest of the month, Diego looks at me like he's got a problem, but he doesn't open his mouth. All he does is stare.

One night he asks if I've cleared my receipts for the day.

He's already found someone to fill in for Miguel. When I get around to talking to him, he isn't all that bad, but he's got his wife and kids down south and this sidechick out in Katy.

She cleans houses, he says. It's good money.

That's who he tells me he's saving for.

12.

About a week before she left, Ma actually sat me down. I'd worked the whole night. Some puto'd spilled oil on my kicks.

She had the windows open by the kitchen sink. A gang of cats posted up on the ledge. Whenever the humidity starts biting, they gather on the fence, and Ma was always knocking the shit out of their tails with her broom.

It'd been a few days since I'd seen her but I knew what was coming. I set a hand on her shoulder and she blinked.

She told me she talked to her sisters. She said they were willing to have me.

I knew I should've been grateful or whatever, but I gave Ma a look.

I said, Well who asked you to do that.

All you have to do is come, she says. You only have to show up.

Nah, I say.

You think I'm lying?

Can't be that simple.

Just show up, Ma said. That's all. You could get a job. They'd have work for a boy like you.

And we'd live happily ever after, I say, in some bum-fuck swamp.

Ma really looked at me then. It was like she hadn't been looking at first, but all of a sudden she was.

You know, she said, you used to be a nice boy.

You and your brother used to be nice boys, she said. Your father, too. All of you nice.

No one could've known you'd turn rotten, she said.

She was quiet while we let that sink in. I know that I should've reached out and hugged her. Pulled on her shoulder. Something physical.

Your brother would've loved it in Louisiana, she said. He'd have loved it. He'd have loved all of the space.

You're reaching.

He'd have loved it.

Javi'd never leave the city.

Maybe, said Ma. But he tried to stay, and look where it got him.

You tell me what you have keeping you here, she said.

Actually, she said, no. You don't have to tell me.

You tell yourself why it is that you're staying, said Ma. When you figure it out, you keep it to yourself.

Ma looks straight at me. It's the most honest face I've ever seen anyone make. A little like she already feels sorry for me. Like she already knows something I don't.

But it's a reason you'll have to live with, she says. Even if it's nothing. And that is something you'll have to live with, too.

13.

I hear knocking at my door and of course it's Miguel. Dude's in the same clothes I saw him in last.

He asks if he can come in, and I say, Fuck no.

We post up in the kitchen.

He sits. I sit.

You gonna offer me something to drink?

Don't give me that faggot shit.

He shrugs.

That mean you're dry?

It means I've got nada and I've got nada for you.

Then I guess I'm fine, says Miguel, after a while, and he rubs his palms over the table.

But there are eggs in the fridge. And they're beside left-over beans from the Castillo. And those sit in some Tupperware, above a flimsy bag of tortillas, so I crack the yolks into something like a scramble and I fry the pinto beans beside them. And I fold the whole thing onto the tortillas, above some slices of avocado, with shredded cheese, and when I tell Miguel that he's SOL for salsa, he doesn't say a word. He's just got this look on his face.

You didn't have to, says Miguel.

You wouldn't have shut up if I hadn't, I say.

I watch Miguel eat and he watches me watch him eat.

It's good, he says.

It's free, I say.

I ask if he's heard from his parents. He doesn't look my way, just keeps chewing his food, but eventually he says that they're fine.

They made it back to their town, he says. But they don't have a phone. They call from the market in the square. All I hear are the fucking roosters.

Sounds like a terrible time, I say.

It's what they know.

Maybe one day they'll wake up.

Maybe.

Miguel runs his fingers across the table.

You think they'll miss it, I say, and he finally looks up at me.

You go somewhere else and stay there and then go back home, he says. Then you tell me how they're feeling.

I just might, I say.

You should've gone with your mother, he says. You're being a pussy. A pato.

Just like you should've flown back to the jungle, I say. But you're here.

I knock on the wood between us.

I'm here, he says, and he raps on it too.

He could still go. Miguel could leave tomorrow. He could pack a suitcase and catch a flight, and I know that I could too. I could pack my shit and ghost. It'd cost nothing at all. But the same way that I know this I know that I probably won't.

I know that even if we don't always do the things that need to be done, we do the things that we need to. I know this the same way that I know Miguel is beside me, in this room, standing where Ma and my father and Javi and Jan have in the years, in the days, before.

Miguel keeps an arm's length away. He peeps the photos on the wall. He asks if the boy in the sweater is my brother.

I could hardly tell, he says, squinting. You don't look anything like him.

Of course we end up upstairs. Neither of us says shit about it. In my bedroom, the one I used to share with Javi, and I don't know how he ends up on top of me but he does.

I'm thinking he'll laugh or smirk or make some kind of crack, but he's got this serious look on his face. And then there's the pressure again. He's shifting his weight, ripping at our sweats.

Está bien?

No, I say.

Really?

No.

This is not how it usually goes for you.

You asking or telling?

When he slips himself inside of me I call him something I don't mean to.

Bueno, says Miguel.

It takes a while. He finishes on my chest. He asks why I'm crying and I tell him I'm not. I tell him to stop bullshitting. Miguel opens his mouth to say something, but he doesn't, just breathes down on my neck, and then I'm hard, again, and then he's back inside of me, but this time it's sweeter, like something that makes sense, but I'm telling him to stop, to leave, to get the fuck out of here, and he's telling me the same, to go, don't come back, and then the words start blending together, and we're saying it in chorus, stop, stop, stop, go on, get out, be gone.

14.

Javi told me no one ever went anywhere they didn't need to.

It was late. East End was dead. He was drunk and fucked-up and locked out. My brother slapped the door, calling my name. Had blood all over his shirt, and I thought he'd gotten his ass beat but when I really gave Javi a look I saw that it didn't belong to him.

He sat on the porch, just looking out at the road.

Ma stayed in bed. I watched him from the window. I felt Jan behind me, leaning on the wall. She wiped at her face, yawning above me.

After a while, I said, You should let him in.

Jan gave me a look, a little like she pitied me.

Listen, she said, if a man's beating on your door this late, you don't let him in. That's the last thing you do.

Serves him right, she said.

Yeah, I said.

He does whatever the fuck he wants.

Yeah.

Leave him, said Jan, I'll let him in later.

I watched her slip back down the hallway.

I opened the door, brought the bowl of menudo we'd picked up for dinner from the stove.

Javi chewed it, quiet as shit. Didn't have any bruises, no scuff marks. He asked if I'd ever thought about leaving Houston and what I did was blink at him.

People think about things all the time, he said. All people fucking do is think.

But really, he said, you do things or you don't.

He reached in his jacket for a cigarette, and then he shook the carton at me.

I didn't smoke and he knew that.

Niggas already know what they'll do, said Javi. They just play like they don't.

I took one anyways. The flame grazed the edge of my chin. We sat smoking, watching Harrisburg, and then he finished his cigarette and stomped that shit out.

15.

The first time I spent the night with a boy, Miguel woke up in my bed the next morning.

He's dark, but not as dark as me. And lanky. And he stinks. But when I watch him snoring on Javi's comforter I don't throw up in my mouth. I don't feel like he's something I have to get rid of.

I squeeze his cheeks, and then his elbows, and then his cheeks again.

A few hours earlier, I woke up to him staring at me. We'd fucked a third time. It couldn't have been later than four. Rain fell just above us, tapping out an ugly melody, and it occurred to me, finally, that I was the last one in this house.

Everyone else was gone. I was the only one left. And when I was gone, that'd be it—that would be the end of our story.

Nic, said Miguel.

What, I said.

Nicolás, said Miguel.

That's my fucking name, I said.

Shit, I said, go to sleep, and I started to roll over, but then Miguel reached across me, squeezing my shoulder.

He pressed his chest against mine, until our noses brushed.

Again? I said.

No, said Miguel.

What if you stayed, he said.

He reached for my arms on the mattress. Laced his

fingers in mine. I could smell me on his breath—or not *me*. Us.

You stink, I said.

Shut up, said Miguel. Listen.

You could leave, he said. I know that. And I know you know.

Pero you don't have to, said Miguel.

We could try, said Miguel.

I want you to think about it, said Miguel. I want you to think about what could happen.

Because I think it could, he said.

And he opened his mouth to say something else and it didn't come out.

Eventually, he fell asleep. But I didn't. I thought about it.

His keys are in the jeans on the floor. I grab my sweats and some sandals. It's still dark when I pull his car out of the neighborhood, and not much brighter when I'm on 59.

I make it out of the Ward. The city's silhouette dims. Its shotguns start thinning, until they're all taquerias and pawnshops and strip clubs. Once I hit Baytown, I'm driving beside the furniture dives, and the pawnshops and junkyards and factories lining the feeder. This is the furthest I've been from the city, my city, in years, but it doesn't feel like anything's changed, and honestly, why would it. You bring yourself wherever you go. You are the one thing you can never run out on.

There's hardly any traffic. The red in the sky turns blue. After like an hour, I'm already in Galveston.

There's a parking lot lining the edge of the beach, this

shitty little pile of gravel. The coast is filled with stragglers, the early morning set. But they don't even look my way. They're figuring out their own shit. I tuck Miguel's keys into the dash. I kick the sandals onto the passenger seat.

I'm like halfway into the water before I finally feel the chill, like one of those whitegirls in the movies. It's the furthest I can get from where I need to be.

Or maybe, just maybe, far enough away from him to actually think, and the sand's like mud on my toes, sweaty with plastic and bottles and grit, but I dig into it anyways. Until it starts to burn.

I pray for my dead in that water.

And I pray for Javi in that water.

And I pray for Jan in that water.

And I pray for Ma in that water.

And I pray for my father in that water.

I start to pray for the boy in my bed but really that nigga should be praying for me. Or maybe his family. We've all got our priorities. And I keep on like that, standing on the shore, muttering and sinking and bobbing, and I hear the water behind me, like this low roar, and then a thumping, like something's getting a little closer. Or I'm getting a little closer. Close to enough to trust him and just give it a go.

And, honestly, I wonder how anyone ever gets away from all that. I used to think that you could.

ACKNOWLEDGEMENTS

Mom and Dad.

Bryce.

Alison and Patrick.

Adam and Rachel and Sanda and Isaac.

Kimberly and Sarah and Analicia and Adrienne and Carlos and Tyson and Joseph.

Adina and Nicole and Silvia and Rebecca and Rachel and Dan and Jason.

Amelia.

Barb and Randy.

Joanna.

Mat.

Katie.

Becky.

The Riverhead crew.

Laura.

Danielle.

David—antes, ahora y después también.